What Is Told

What Is Told

ASKOLD MELNYCZUK

Faber and Faber

BOSTON • LONDON

First published in 1994 in the United States by Faber and Faber,
Inc., 50 Cross Street, Winchester, MA 01890.

Library of Congress Cataloging-in-Publication Data

Melnyczuk, Askold.
    What is told : a novel / by Askold Melnyczuk.
        p.   cm.
    ISBN 0-571-19830-9 (cloth)
    1. Ukrainian Americans—New Jersey—History—Fiction.
2. Family—New Jersey—Fiction.   I. Title.
PS3563.E445W48   1994
813'.54—dc20   93-42837
                                                          CIP

Jacket design by Adrian Morgan at Red Letter Design
Jacket photograph by Elisabet Zeilon

Printed in the United States of America

For my parents, Edward and Olena,
and for my sister, Hannusia

"Is there anything truer than truth? Yes, legend. This gives eternal meaning to ephemeral truth."

Kazantzakis, *Report to Greco*

"On any given evening, peasants in outlying villages might also be found gathered around campfires or in low wooden huts to hear storytellers sing or recite from memory the timeless folk and epic heroic tales. These *starina* ("what is told"), handed down by oral tradition from generation to generation, father to son, told of the stalwart warriors of Kiev who with their mighty sword-strokes had split their foes in two . . . "

B. Bobrick, *Ivan the Terrible*

CAST

Toor Zabobon, *king of the Rozdorizhans*
Olha, *his wife*
Cyril, *his brother*

Zenon Zabobon, *professor of art history in Rozdorizha*
Natalka, *his wife*
Stefan, *his brother*
Slava Lastivka, *daughter of Zenon and Natalka*

Arkady Vorog, *husband of Slava*
Bohdan, *their son*

Edward Zaremba, *a cousin*

Kopf, *foreman at the SeaLand Plant*

Dr. William Kaiser, *a neighbor*

Gwen McDonald, *a neighbor*

A thousand relatives

Seafarers

Woman Is the Future

In 1914 Zenon Zabobon, a professor of art history at the men's gymnasium in Rozdorizha, refused a job as curator of the Scythian collection at the London Museum of Archaeology because, he explained in a letter to his younger brother Stefan, he was in love. Stefan replied: "Stupid to toss a career for a vooman, *mon frère.*" Stefan was a student at the university in Vienna where, rumor claimed, he maintained a modest seraglio. Zenon did not listen. He adored the dark-eyed, opulent Natalka. Moreover, she needed his help. She was new to the city and had far too many suitors. Men crowded the bakery for a box of the pastries she clumsily webbed with string. Without Zenon, she'd wind up a barmaid, or worse. Their marriage would be more than a personal blessing: it would be a public service.

When Stefan learned of the decision, he wrote in his journal: "My brother is an idiot. More proof he takes after Father's side of the family. The Zabobons have no instinct about marriage."

Stefan's journal bulged with ideas for myriad projects, including *Notes Toward a Theory of Marriage*; entries from an essay on *The Metaphysics of Travel*; and copious hermetic jottings toward his most ambitious scheme, a history in which events that occurred in his native city of Rozdorizha were juxtaposed against what happened at the same time elsewhere in the world. In 1492, for example, Columbus landed in Cuba, Da Vinci sketched the first flying machine, and Rurik Zabobon slew his neighbor's cow, fueling a feud that was to last three centuries.

They married the day Archduke Ferdinand was shot in Sarajevo. It was a steamy afternoon toward the end of June. Day lilies decked the altar.

"Why do people marry in such weather?" the priest grumbled, as he slipped his cassock on over his robes.

At first nobody seemed to notice the archduke's death. The Hungarian stock exchange rose several points. Weeks passed before the Austrians decided it was time to show Serbia what was what. Emperor Franz Josef said, "If the monarchy must end, let that end be glorious."

Zenon soon found himself waging war on two fronts.

Natalka was the model of Ukrainian womanhood. All she needed was an education. That would be his job. He lectured her, flourishing his bifocals like a baton. A progressive, Zenon believed in the emancipation of women. He wanted an equal, one he himself had created.

Natalka didn't know what to expect from marriage. She knew only what she'd learned from watching her parents. The couple worked the fields for Polish landlords. All day they ploughed, planted, scythed. At night they screamed at each other. They celebrated truces by collapsing together onto the straw-stuffed mattress.

Their negotiations produced twelve boys and girls who slept doubled and tripled on pallets laid out on the floor of the one-room cottage. Natalka's mother controlled her brood with a remedy of poppy seeds boiled in milk. The formula was so effective that most of them drank several glasses a day for the rest of their lives.

Natalka seemed a changeling even to her parents. She was beautiful, feckless, eccentric. She liked embracing sunflowers, planting her big mouth smack on their seeds. She was prone to wandering off by herself into the forest, where wild boar growled in the bushes and where she listened so earnestly to the low whisper of wind in the pines that the trees wondered what she expected of them. Her mother scolded her frequently and had regular recourse to the pedagogical strap.

Natalka neither felt the blows nor heard the lectures. It was as though she were intercepting the radio waves that had begun to flutter between the great cities of the world. A gypsy fortune-teller she visited noticed her long fingers and predicted she'd become a concert pianist, playing Vienna, Paris, London.

"And you will go to New York."

"Where is New York?"

The world beyond the village was all rumor. Only Uncle Yarko, who lived with the chickens, knew about it. Scattering feed, he babbled about cities where the sun never set, where rivers flowed inside houses so that people swam in their rooms and later drove down the streets in buckets with wheels. All this the girl, against her better judgment, believed.

For the next four years she hunted for a piano. Once, an accordionist and a blind *bandurist* stopped in the village. The tubercular accordionist let the girl run her fingers across the keys while he primed the instrument. The sound was unlike anything she'd ever heard.

"It's like a piano?" she offered.

He laughed. He said it was as much like a piano as the bark of a dog was like the patter of an angel. But that was plenty for him since he spent a lot more time with dogs than with angels.

She fell in love with Zenon's voice first. His face was blurred by thick bifocals. He was a conservative dresser who favored blue suits with matching bow ties. Everywhere he went he lugged an attaché case bursting with books and papers. She didn't care what was in them. But his voice when he ordered pastries was half growl and half chant. It reminded her of the forest. She cared less about what he said, about his wild ideas, his rants about the noble savage and the wisdom of the peasantry, or the importance of nationalism. Gnarling a string around his box of cookies, she listened, but not to his words.

———

Zenon had many passions, including Lord Byron and day lilies. He believed his country needed to free itself from the influence of its neighbors — Russia and Poland and Austria. It needed to keep alive the purity of its native tongue. The language would live, he told Natalka, because of people like her: she was the national treasure.

He asked her to sing the songs she learned from her

mother. He wanted to record them for the sake of their grandchildren, for history.

Natalka hated the maudlin melodies—the laments about girls left by their lovers, or the crowing of cossacks. She preferred the new music that drifted out of cafés in the student quarters.

There was a song about cranes he made her sing over and over while he lay in her lap, dreaming of freedom. Natalka raked her fingers through his sparse hair. She remembered her mother shouting at her father while her brothers and sisters smiled from their milky opium dreams.

After their honeymoon she moved into his apartment. The four rooms were high-ceilinged, with mahogany moldings and a large stove in the kitchen that heated the quarters through the long winters. Ihor, the idiot deaf-mute brother Zenon had nursed since their mother's death, lived with them.

One morning Natalka discovered Ihor playing with himself. She smacked him with a pillow. Ihor smiled. When she understood her husband expected her to take care of him, she screamed. She was not a maid. She had not come to the city to live the way her mother had lived. Who did he think she was? Why was he always trying to change her? She liked herself well enough without his books and his theories, thank you, and if he didn't, well, he could leave. Or she would. Why was he constantly telling her what to think about God and motherhood and her country when she grasped these things perfectly well without him?

Natalka's sphere of influence was bounded by the

walls of the bedroom. There Zenon suffered his worst defeats.

On the other hand, Zenon thought to himself as he paced the late night streets after an argument, she had many redeeming qualities. She was honest and pragmatic and knew how to handle the butcher. Jadviga, his mother's old cook, respected her. His wife mocked his homilies about peasant life, but she made sure he had his veal and tomatoes and his clean shirts with starched collars. She sewed her own clothes. She was pretty, long-lashed, plump. So what if she cared nothing for the story of King Toor and the founding of Rozdorizha?

———

The Zabobons had lived in Rozdorizha for over a thousand years before War finally insisted they move on. They were hard, stubborn people, and there was a popular saying that they would leave town only after the mountains swam down the river to the Black Sea. But War was tougher. War was a god.

There had been earlier wars and invasions. Over the centuries, the town's burial grounds had swelled. Skeletons, paler than apple cores, clamored, "More room! More room!" To quiet them, the living cropped farmland and cleared acres of forest.

The dead would not stay dead. They rose, their rotten bodies battered with blood and dirt, and stumbled through the village, tormenting their petrified kin.

None of this frightened Toor. King Toor Zabobon slept wrapped up in clouds he pulled from the sky each night. He talked to the wind and was on fair terms with the rain. He paid no mind to the omens that worried his people. Why brood about a crow chewing on a human heart, or a plague of frogs that turned the golden steppes into a writhing green sea?

Neither was Toor afraid of the Tartars. When they appeared, he was waiting. Tall as five spears set end to end, with fingers of iron, legs of bronze, he had been bred for battle. He called the Tartars barbarians and rebuffed their salvo of arrows.

He remembered his origins. What distinguished him from his cousins, the trees, on which he sat in meditative moments, was that he could walk while they could not. It was a mixed blessing, because a man who knew how to walk soon learned how to run away. A tree, meanwhile, had no choice but to stay put. He felt a fealty to these first citizens, the poplars, mulberries, and pines. Poplars gave buds he used in preparing a salve for burns and hemorrhoids. An extract from pine bark relieved his diarrhea. Even the willows cooperated, offering leaves which he boiled to cure his insomnia. He would never abandon such friends.

To defend them he commanded the front line of battle. He sailed his sword through the Tartars. They replied by chopping off his right arm. Sweating fire, he hoisted his spear and hurled it, skewering a line of these sons of Hagar. He strode to where they stood, yanked it clean. He drew his sword, buffed it with ox hide, and marched up the row, systematically beheading each man. After piling the six heads in a heap, he knelt for the detail work, trimming ears, noses, scalps, peeling skin, paring flesh. Blood flowed from his shoulder while he scrubbed and rinsed the skulls in the river. Then he poked a vine through the eye sockets of the two largest ones and, slinging them over his neck, sauntered over to a crowd celebrating round a huge fire.

"We won," the crowd cried, shaking their ragged heads.

"Don't I know! Pour some wine into these," he insisted.

"Where did you get them?" they asked, filling the skulls.

As Toor recounted the battle, one cried, "They cut off your arm!"

"Yes, there it is," someone else pointed. And, indeed, inside the flames of the towering fire stood his right arm, its fingers flickering like five tallow candles. He laughed, swilling wine.

The Political World

WHILE ZENON agreed with much of Marx, especially with the fundamentals of the labor theory of value and the parts of *Das Kapital* that outlined the mystical properties of matter and its propensity for enslaving humanity; and while he paid close attention to news of the revolutionary activity around St. Petersburg, he was himself the offspring of generations of priests (there were other branches on the family tree, including politicians and pimps and generals, but he disregarded these anomalies, preferring to trace his lineage to King Toor's brother Cyril, the priest). His nationalism and his religious convictions were deep. He belonged to the Shevchenko Scientific Society. When the Ukrainian language was again suppressed by the Russians, who had recently seized Rozdorizha, he published an article about Scythian pottery and its influence on Galician folk art. The Russians responded to this outburst by arresting Zenon and the journal's editors.

In the twilight years, between the czarist regime and the communist state, Governor Chuj decided to restructure the region's cultural life. His dispensation required the suppression of all bourgeois inclinations. The ambitious and bewildering program inspired mass paranoia. People were discouraged from taking an interest in local history. Instead they were told to attend meetings at which they could declare their loyalty to the czar. The order drove people crazy. Lifelong neighbors accused each other of crimes against the state. Intellectuals and nationalists were found everywhere, among butchers and milkmen and idiots. Naturally the Jews suffered.

The police became convinced Ihor, the deaf-mute, was a spy. No one bothered to mention for whom they thought he was working. The police had a job to do. One afternoon they burst into the Zabobon apartment. Ihor sat in the corner playing with the cat, stroking its erect tail. When he failed to reply to their questions, they kicked and beat him. Natalka screamed. She raced into the kitchen, where the cook cowered behind the black stove. She grabbed a knife and hurried back into the living room. But the police had already gone, taking Ihor with them.

Released from prison, Zenon did all he could to track down his brother. But there was no record of the arrest.

A few months later the governor and the Russians were forced out of Galicia by the Germans.

One day Lenin was sighted in Zurich; the next, in St. Petersburg. Gossip claimed the Romanovs were done for. Other rumors insisted they were stronger than ever. Austria verged on surrender. It was in command and promised Galicia independence. And in the fall of 1917, Austria and Germany performed a miracle: they resurrected Poland.

Around the same time, Natalka learned she was pregnant, and Captain Zenon Zabobon, of the Galician army, was reported shot.

He had been shot by the Poles. Or the Russians. No one was certain. The Ukrainians seemed to switch alliances weekly. The man who informed Natalka arrived at the house at two in the morning, wearing civilian clothes, a gray fedora pushed back on his head like a cossack cap, his left hand in the pocket of a gray overcoat. He did not stay to comfort her.

Frantic, Natalka consulted the three people in the city she still trusted. Everyone else she'd known had either left the country or been arrested. Her friends shrugged and squeezed her hand sympathetically: what could they do? They knew no more than she did about the several ongoing wars.

Natalka developed a fever. Head throbbing, she took to her bed. She refused to rise even when Jadviga the cook begged her to visit Doctor Hlib—who himself was too busy to attend to depressed ladies. "It's only grief," he counseled the cook. "She'll sleep it off."

She slept. When she opened her eyes, she still did not feel awake. She began talking to herself. She cursed the czar. Lying there, a quilt edged with black crosses tucked under her neck, she swore revenge against the Serbian prince. She would kill every last archduke on earth. Who did these men think they were that she should lose a husband for their sakes?

Natalka glared at Zenon's books. How had their wisdom helped anyone? Why had he wasted his life reading when they could not even stop a bullet? Wasn't he always shouting about miracles, the miracle of Italy, the miracle of France, the miracle of Germany, even the miracle of Russia . . .

She forced herself out of bed and attacked the library with scissors.

By day's end, the collection of a lifetime had been snipped into a pile of pale worms. Satisfied, she got back into bed.

Months passed. Her belly swelled until it looked like she had swallowed the moon. In October she had a change of heart. She moved through the apartment in a kind of trance, acknowledging to the objects around her that, even without her husband, she intended to live.

Good, sang the chair. *Good,* echoed the curtains. *Good,* thought King Toor.

One afternoon, as the cook prepared to leave for her sister's across town, Natalka cried, "I think it's now."

Jadviga dropped her suitcase, slipped off her coat, and waddled back into the kitchen.

Later she folded a green woolen blanket into the washbasin and turned it into a crib for the baby girl she had delivered.

The child would never hear her father's stories about the early days of their city.

———

Need kept soul and body linked and limber. The Tartars mowed down thousands, but the Rozdorizhans grew back, nearly overnight, like the wheat that was their staple crop. The village lay in what later came to be called Ukraine, near what later came to be called Poland, at the crossroads of two great rivers. The ranks of the antiphonal choir of profit and trade were always swelling.

The day after the attack the villagers began rebuilding. Within months it was business as usual: men and women sweated in the fields, the elders bickered in the square, drunks drooled in the tavern, and the madman in the forest recited dogma to wormwood. Market Square echoed with the cries of rug weavers, beet farmers, silversmiths: all the coarse and passionate clamor of business.

The rivers were named Nebo and Peklo, Heaven and Hell (literally *sky* and *hot place*). Heaven was wide and mild and rarely rose above its mossy banks, while Hell brimmed and flooded easily, claiming scores of victims every year.

Every morning Toor bathed near the bridge where the rivers met. He waded into the Nebo, leaned across the spit of land separating the bodies of water, dipped his hand into the misty Peklo, ladled up the water, and slurped. Then he would lie on his back and let the current drag him to the rivers' juncture, which, at high tide, whirled with maelstroms. He bobbed in the water, gazing at the fogged sky. How long had he been doing this? A hundred years? Twenty? Silver and green fish leaped from the water and a crane stitched the mist, slipping inside a patch of cloud. He shut his eyes and, in a light sleep, dreamed he'd wakened in another world where the people were tiny and the large houses had sprouted silvery branches. Now he saw his wife Olha rise naked from the water and come toward him and now he heard her voice from far away crying that he had a visitor.

By the time he reached his hut he was dry. He bent down and kissed his wife, who was shearing the vegetable lamb. Then he turned to the scrawny, hairless boy who stood nearby, blood welting his feet. He'd run twenty *versts* through the forest to warn Toor the Tartars had just burned down eight villages.

The vegetable lamb grazed calmly while Olha's long fingers moved through its smoke-colored locks. She pinched the thick tufts fondly. She'd grown the lamb from seed and remembered well the days when it was no more than a dandelion-sized sprout with tiny hooves that nervously tapped the ground. It bleated, swaying its stalk, and stretched its neck toward the grass rimming the circle it had nibbled. The lamb moved slowly. Once this grass was gone, it would begin to die.

"Sharpen your spears!" Toor cried, hearing the horses just before he saw them emerge from the woods, a forest of furs on the warpath. Frightened, the villagers looked to Toor, who fisted two spears in one hand. He ordered the people to hide themselves behind the wooden palisade surrounding the village.

He stood alone in the open gateway. What was it these barbarians wanted? He'd overheard a Tartar say once: May you abide in one place continually, like a Christian, and inhale your own stink.

As soon as he could smell the horses, he signaled his men; arrows whiskered the air and fell pell-mell on the enemy. He chucked the spears. No second thoughts: act, fight.

He was in the thick of it, across the river near the forest, when word reached him an arrow had hit Olha.

He hurried toward her but the enemy kept rising up

in his way. By the time he arrived she was dead. Their dog guarded her body. The vegetable lamb lay on its back, feet up, the stalk rising from its belly spurting green.

He bent to kiss her lips. Then he rose. He howled. Lunatic, he raced back to the front.

He was the wind exploding in a field. He moved so fast the Tartars couldn't see him and they fled.

Toor returned, salted with arrows, to find the body laid out on a slab of stone at the village gate.

He lifted his wife in his arm and wept. For three days he cried. His tears wore a river into the earth. The people named it the Olha.

The Near-Death Society

OUTSIDE, a November rain pelted the slate roof, spraying out copper spouts, onto the cobblestones. Inside, Natalka wept as she looked down at the fatherless babe tucked in her bassinet.

The child gurgled and yowled, flailing her possum hands in rage and smiling candidly at moths and mothers and cooks. She cared nothing for the ancient and historical grievances occupying the giants.

Natalka considered taking the girl to her parents' in Nizhne, but a memory of her drunken father's shoes sticking out from under the table blotted the impulse.

"We're the loneliest women in Rozdorizha," she said.

Lately she craved those Dutch chocolates shaped like clogs which Jadviga the cook discovered in a small store near the church. (Fact: they lived on ration coupons. Fact: Jadviga regularly bought pricey chocolates. How?) A voice inside screeched *More! More!*

How to support her child? She hadn't worked a day since quitting the bakery. The city was peopled by strangers. Zenon's friends had all been shot or deported. The few still alive were in hiding.

She thought of her brother-in-law, Stefan, who

brought them fortune cookies when he came through last year. What a curious man, with his monocle and the dolphin-handled cane. His manners were as puzzling as his clothes. His gestures were fraught with flourishes and his speech with fragments of phrases she didn't understand (every time he was introduced to a woman he clicked his heels, bowed, and said something that sounded like *Eggs today!*). He seemed eager to make people like him. The rumors surrounding him, however, were awful: people whispered he was a traitor, that he was good friends with Levin or Lenin or whoever that bearded man was, but her husband had ignored the gossip, saying that people didn't know what they were talking about, that his brother had troubles of his own which had nothing to do with politics.

Maybe he could help her.

She found his address among the stack of letters on Zenon's desk. She asked her neighbor to write the letter for her.

The note reached the embassy weeks later and was forwarded to Madame Poprovska's, where Stefan had become a semipermanent house guest.

———

After his wife's death, King Toor called a village meeting.

There had been a battle in Heaven, he explained. The old gods had lost their powers. Someone had stolen Perun's thunder.

"Who has done this?" the people asked.

"The new God."

"How do you know this, Toor?"

"Why do you think we've suffered so? We pray, make offerings, kill fat sheep. What difference does it make? The Tartars keep coming. It's because we're praying to the losers."

To prove it, he asked Stash, the blacksmith, to bring the clay statuette of Perun, the chief god.

"Here is Perun, thunder-maker," he cried, waving the figurine above his head.

Wind rippled through his cloud of beard. A chicken squawked. Mamaliga, the village soothsayer, farted. Everyone eyed the figure suspended above his head.

He cast it down, and it burst like a cup.

No one moved.

Toor stared wildly, afraid he'd gone too far, while his dog loped up and licked his blood-caked knee. Then the sun glanced through the clouds. It was the sign he'd been waiting for.

"See," he shouted, "Nothing! Nothing! The gods are gone. They're dead."

A voice ventured timidly, "Then who is up there?"

"Someone new!" Toor declared.

The people waited for more, but he fell silent, suddenly tongue-tied, blinking at the crowd.

Truth was, he didn't know. But he remembered the Tartar's crack about the Christians. Anything these monkeys on greyhounds hated had to be a good thing. He'd been asking around. His younger brother Markian had sailed the hundred rivers to Byzantium to observe this Christian business first hand. He'd told Toor about the Man-God (or was it God-Man? —the distinction puzzled him) who came to earth and wrestled with Death and won. "What did he do then?" Toor asked.

"Cut off Death's head and planted it on a spear," Markian embroidered. "But," he added, "the God-Man later insisted the killing stop." This soothed the weary fighter.

Toor's wife sometimes returned in dreams. She said she waited for him on the other side. He believed the new God could carry him there. But how could he win the support of the people? He was a fighter, not a politician.

"I am going for a swim. Then I will take an important nap during which I must not be disturbed," he said, gesturing his brother forward. "Markian will explain."

This inspiration further proved the new God's power.

He ambled down to the Olha, peeled off his cloak, and slipped in. A legion of dragonflies zipped aside to let him pass. He was floating on his back, jetting water, cold to the copperheads glancing off the backs of his knees and to the cranes in the reeds eyeing him when his younger brother Cyril saw him and waved.

Cyril was late for the village meeting. He'd had a vision the night before which he wished to share with his neighbors; moreover, along the way he'd seen three crows in a tree. It was a sign only Mamaliga, the soothsayer, could explain. He swept the sweat off his forehead and hobbled down the hill, his clubfoot dragging.

———

One gray afternoon Natalka returned from a walk in the park with her baby to find Zenon sprawled across the blue armchair, smoking his pipe, looking out the window.

Tears filled her eyes. She thought at last she'd be able to make it up to her husband for having been such a bad pupil. She wanted to smooth her hair, paint her eyes. She wanted to sing the song about the cranes. Instead, she raced toward him.

Their kiss was brief. The baby began to cry and Natalka had to turn away.

"What's her name?" he asked softly.

"Slava Lastivka."

From then on they called her Lastivka, which means sparrow.

He took the child in his arms. His wife pressed her hands to his cheeks and ran them along his shoulders.

"Yes, there was a bullet there," he said. "And there."

He stared at the child, bewildered at how life had borne the fruits of his desires even without him. He looked at Natalka and thought she'd aged a little in his absence: there were gray hairs, and the lips that used to kiss the sunflowers seemed paler than before.

———

He'd been taken out with the other prisoners at dawn. He'd wondered what his wife was doing, whether the baby was a boy or a girl, what would happen to his precious library (Natalka's heart still pounded at the word). His shirt itched and he wanted to scratch himself, but his hands were tied behind his back. After the rifles had fired and everyone had fallen—he had dropped down right along with them, assuming that he'd been hit—he lay there thinking how trite it was for hell to smell like piss and shit. He heard a noise a few feet away. One of the corpses sat up. Their eyes met. "Polish sharpshooters," the man observed.

Why hadn't he let her know he was alive?

"Because it was dangerous," he explained. He had to wait till the Germans left.

Natalka studied the silver moth circling the electric lamp.

His voice was the same, yet this wasn't the man she'd sung to six months before.

Quieter, more remote, he spent his days staring out the window. At first he did not even trouble to replace his library. But in time he noticed that he missed his books the way some men missed people, and over the years the shelves were resettled with new volumes. He no longer acted the missionary, however: he no longer flailed his bifocals, telling Natalka what to think and feel. His movements seemed catlike, mindful, and gentler, as though the world were fragile as a nest twined of bird bones and lace. Natalka complained to a neighbor that she hardly recognized him. Every so often he asked her to sing the song about the cranes but when he tried nestling his head in her lap, she flinched. He let even this pass without comment.

There were things about his execution he couldn't discuss with Natalka.

Most stories of near-death experiences mention a journey down a tunnel. Light rims the blackness at the end. Gradually a feeling of calm descends: God is Love.

One's hours of soul searching seem presumptuous: God is Love. The rest is that ridiculous misunderstanding that goes by the name of history.

Survivors are changed. Revenants speak of being born again, finding analogies for their experience in the Buddhist's promise not to enter Nirvana until the whole world is ready for the journey. Moreover, they feel a thirst, actually a physical need, to associate with others who've gone down the same road.

There were many such fellow travelers in Rozdorizha at this time. Somehow they found each other, recognizing here a look, there a gesture. Eventually they coalesced into an informal fraternity they dubbed the Near-Death Society. The group met monthly in some inconspicuous place, a café run by Germans or Hungarians, where no one understood Ukrainian. A stranger glancing at the table might have imagined a reunion of high school classmates, or a cabal of trade unionists.

Zenon attended regularly. The group gave him a forum where he could speak about the most important moment in his life. He detailed *the* morning: crisp, five degrees Celsius. He could smell cut hay and manure. He hadn't eaten a thing. He remembered the song he hummed to himself: the one about the cranes. Foremost in his mind had been Natalka, his mother, and Mrs. Glick—by that time everyone knew she had been his father's mistress though it wasn't from her he had contracted syphilis.

And a feeling of clarity. The way he'd lived was just one way among many. He was as right in his convictions as the men who were about to shoot him. That, and a spasm of longing for another hour of sensual experience, one last hour of life in the body.

Others confirmed the rush of erotic desire. Oka Pavlichko giggled, telling the group how the first thing she did on returning to "civilization" was take a lover. To hell with what her mother said. The meetings helped Zenon steer his course. And the experience renewed his faith in the importance of keeping alive the old tales, which were truer than the stories in the papers.

———

The people built a barge sturdy enough to carry Markian and Cyril to Byzantium. The day before their departure, the women cooked up roast swan and spiced crane, which they served along with endless barrels of wine and beer. The villagers drank, danced, sang.

The soothsayer Mamaliga refused to join in. She skulked near the poplars, crying, "Idiots! You'll see! Perun's alive and thriving! You've forgotten your true gods! Your children will be born with the heads of dogs!"

A foot drove her to the ground. "Better leave while you have legs. Witch!"

"I won't. This is my home."

"Oh no?"

Someone ripped off her sack, exposing rootlike teats, while the dog howled outside the door of the empty cottage.

Hours later she dragged herself to the woods. She curled up at the foot of an oak. Kissing its roots, she begged the gods to punish the Rozdorizhans.

When the village roused from its stupor, Markian and Cyril were aboard the barge, set to sail.

Before boarding, Cyril himself sought out the knottier, who controlled the weather with his bundle of ropes.

"Show me your hands," he said.

The fat man complied.

Cyril pulled out his sword and swiftly loped the hands off at the wrists.

"Now try freeing the storms," he barked.

Red-eyed and parched, the Rozdorizhans waved good-bye, then sank back to sleep.

Every Sunday after mass, Zenon took his daughter with him to the cemetery, where he placed a white lily on his mother's grave. This gesture bore strange fruit: Lastivka developed an appetite for the scenery. When she was old enough to go out on her own, she retraced their steps down streets leading straight to her grandmother's grave. It became her favorite hideaway. She climbed the willow near the pond, tested the doors of the Blud Mausoleum, fed the geese, befriended the squirrels. Summers she lay amid the stones, reading children's stories and later poetry and newspapers in which she especially favored obituaries. The girl had a collection of pressed flowers gathered from the various cemeteries—Ukrainian, Polish, and Jewish. Over the years she supplemented it with a collection of butterflies, moths, and rocks also gleaned from the graveyards.

Her mother tried to interest the child in the piano.

"Because your father wants you to, that's why," Natalka said.

Her teacher, though blind, could play *Für Elise* with his nose. "To play the piano, my poor, incompetent friend," he said to his hapless pupil, "You must play with your whole body and not just, as you do, with your nose."

He bent down and nosed out several bars of Beethoven. When Natalka came to take Lastivka home, he grabbed for the old girl's buttocks but was slapped away.

Natalka shook her head. Piano lessons! The girl had no idea how lucky she was. She prayed the lessons would continue.

———

Years later, Toor and his people awoke in time to help Cyril build the church.

Trees were cut, dragged up hill, cut again, planed. Even the knot-tier, whose hands had grown back long before, put his fleshy shoulder to the wheel. Semen the tailor was leading his horse, Old Stribunetz, to the river for a drink and didn't hear Stash shout, "Ho! The tree!" It took three men to roll the oak off. The horse was still flapping his lips, a brown eye lolling in its socket, when Stash brought down the axe.

Everyone asked about their journey in search of the new God.

"It is a wonderful and terrifying place beyond the forests," observed Markian. "We killed many dragons and we finally met the Obs, who live not far south of here. They die each autumn and come back each spring."

He invented, stole stories gleaned from other travelers. The people listened greedily, gripped by news of the life outside, proud to learn they lived in an oasis of culture and light, and that they were wise to stay home, in the womb of civilization.

One dawn Cyril donned his white robe, with its crosses and Greek letters (alpha, omega) stitched in gold, and tugged the bell rope outside the church.

The entire village crammed in.

Cyril snapped orders: "Men to one side, women to the other. Little boy, come here. Now silence."

After the bewildering, four-hour service, he told the people they were to come see him three times a week.

"Why so often?" Stash asked.

"To help you remember," Cyril explained. The robes gave him courage.

"Remember what?"

"What you did to me last night," cried a woman from across the room.

"And that's not even his wife," a stranger added.

"Who'll feed the horses?" Stash persisted.

So the dialogue went.

Some rejected the new God immediately. Babies kept dying; teeth rotted; spouses took lovers. Many refused to confess their secrets to Cyril. Yet most were smitten by the novel ritual and by as much of the doctrine as they were able to make out from Cyril's sermons, which each week grew increasingly intricate.

The Almighty Kopek

THOUGH HE no longer discussed politics with his family, Zenon remained obsessed with his country's fate. On January 22, 1919, the eastern and western parts of the land were united by the rebel Petliura. By February 4, the Bolsheviks were in Kiev. First Rozdorizha was independent and Ukrainian; then it was subject and Polish. And then Soviet. When a colleague of his at the high school, a Pole who taught geography, asked him why this nationalist business mattered so much to him—because a glance at maps of the region from the last millennium proved how absurd any side's claims to supremacy in the area might be—Zenon took off his bifocals and was about to launch into a lecture. But he caught himself. He put his glasses back on, smiled, and replied courteously that if their positions were reversed and he found himself a Pole in a predominantly Ukrainian world, well, he might feel differently. Anyway, Zenon pointed out, since Poland was alive again, he could afford not to care.

Years passed in a stupor of gunfire and revolution.

Zenon wrote letters on behalf of political prisoners, smuggling messages back and forth between them and their families, the letters and journals inscribed on cigarette papers passed during exchanges of smokes, or via a guard bribed with vodka and blood sausages.

"It's not our fault the country's come to this," his brother Stefan said during a brief trip home. As usual, his appearance was cloaked in scandal and rumor: he was a courier for the Ukrainian Central Government in Kiev or an informant for the decimated Mensheviks or Trotsky's secret adviser. "It's this stupid country itself," he explained. "It's a hydra: one body and a hundred heads telling it what to do."

The point is, Stefan confided in his journal, *we are all marginal figures, shoved to the periphery of events by history. Even our cause seems ludicrous: whoever writes our story will be telling the tale of the hunt from the hare's point of view.*

There were summers, too. Despite the guns. To spite them, maybe. Middle-class families managed to leave the city for the resorts, where they swam and took baths and drank mineral water.

Natalka understood how bad things were getting when the nightmare followed her to the spa. She suffered a recurring dream in which she and Lastivka were taken up in an air balloon operated by a man with side whiskers and a pince-nez. When the earth looked marble-small, he asked them if they knew how to fly. Any minute the balloon would be turned upside down. Lastivka screamed. Natalka grabbed a pair of scissors and lunged at him. Before she could reach him, he disappeared and the blade entered the balloon, which swung violently. The sky above them blackened with singing clouds. Natalka heard their singing, but she couldn't make out the words. Then the balloon was wafted up by a gust and she and her daughter shaken out like salt into the sea below. Just as they were about to break against the waves, the clouds, still singing, swooped down under them, and they landed on the feathers of a million singing cranes who lifted them into a sky now thick with dirigibles. Natalka, calmer, saw a mountain on the horizon and standing on it, a man. Covered with hair, a tree almost, he waved his one arm. Then the cranes did a nose dive, letting the women fall.

She told her daughter about the dream. The girl laughed and asked, "Mother, have you ever heard a name as funny as this: Johann Galsworty?"

"I never read books."

"I know. But you'd like this anyway. It's about love in a place very far away. In England."

"I have heard of England. But I have never been there. Shakespeere. It's the country that made him."

"And Oskar Weeld-e."

"It is a barbaric place, my darling. Anglo-Saxons are very cruel. I almost went there to study piano." She sighed, overwhelmed by her own fantasies. Natalka was not a reader and her imagination ran wild. She had no way of knowing which of the notions that slipped into her head were probable and which absurd. Everything seemed possible: if she saw no monsters around her, that did not mean they weren't *somewhere*—in an uncharted part of the globe, in France, or America. Can we imagine what Emma Bovary's inner life might have been like had she never cracked open a book?

Markian became keeper of the book, a post as puzzling to the people as Cyril's priestcraft.

"What do you put in it?" Stash asked.

"Everything," Markian insisted.

He meant it. People said if you wanted to know how many blades of grass sprouted in the cemetery behind the new church, ask Markian.

This writing business rattled the Rozdorizhans. How was it possible for men to translate themselves, their very essence, the breath that rose from their bellies, into berry drippings on parchment? Powerful magic. A scroll of writing could put a man into a trance, changing his body into a vessel for another's dreams. According to Markian, it was by this magic a man might live forever—a notion Cyril disputed.

These ideas tormented Stash. He longed to see, even fondle, the mystic markings.

One night while the scribe was helping neighbors with a mill pond, Stash, who seemed to spend less and less time at the smithy, stole into Markian's house.

He stood over the table where the subtle parchments lay tied with leather laces when behind him a woman's voice whispered in a language he'd never heard before. It was Olha, Toor's wife! He froze. A rat raced between his legs. Two cheeks of wind whistled through the straw roof.

Forgetting the prayers Cyril taught him, he begged Perun, host of thunder, to help. Floorboards creaked, cloth rustled. The spirit drew closer. Trembling, he raced for the door and ran out. He burned a calf to Perun and cursed himself for rejecting the old gods. He never did touch the scrolls, whose number multiplied daily.

In them one could read how Taras seduced his sister and then the offspring of that branch gradually withered into whores and drunkards; how fourteen-year-old Darka, caught by Tartars, led her captors into the woods, then tricked them into trying to cross the Chorne Ozero, which was quicksand, and most of them drowned. A communal diary, Markian's scrolls (which people referred to as *the* book) helped settle arguments. If, generations later, no one quite believed that Cyril—locally dubbed a saint—had once walked the waters of the roiling Peklo or that he'd said mass for a week with a Tartar arrow piercing his heart before being dragged up to Heaven by a pair of blond angels, if no one wholly accepted these tales, people nevertheless agreed they conveyed fundamental truths.

The role of keeper of the book was passed down through generations of Zabobons. After Markian came Andrew and after Andrew, Askold and after Askold, Darko, and so on *in saeculae saeculorum* . . .

Several scrolls were devoted to speculations about Toor's disappearance. No one knew what happened. One day he never came back from his afternoon swim. That evening divers poked long sticks down miles of riverbed, and fishermen dragged their nets across every accessible inch of the Nebo and the Peklo. But it was as though Toor had been wafted up to the sky by dragonflies or dissolved in the bracing eddies of the Olha. Rumor claimed he'd gone on a pilgrimage to the Holy

Land. Or that Perun, the lost god of thunder, had changed him to a snake.

Zenon supplemented his teaching duties by working on several relief committees organized to send food to eastern parts of the country.

On the ward at St. Cyril's Hospital, where he also volunteered, he observed frequent cases of malnutrition.

"What's happening in the East, brother?" he asked one of the patients.

"There's no food. No food. All shipped to the cities."

But the areas where this was happening were sealed off, and news reached other towns slowly. One patient told him about a black market in human flesh. He claimed to have visited a store where trays of human limbs, organs, fingers, cheeks, noses, toes, and so on were stacked behind the counters.

Impossible, Zenon thought, rubbing his temples. To scrape the flesh out of a human cheek? What could he do? Over months he heard more: entire villages turned cannibal; trains carrying tourists had been attacked, children boiled alive.

The news from America was also puzzling. The stock market had crashed. Gangsters ran the country. The new capital of the United States was Chicago; the new president, Signore Capone. Yet Hollywood kept sending films: he and Natalka howled over the exploits of Laurel and Hardy and Charlie Chaplin, while Natalka nurtured a crush on Robert Donat, and Lastivka screamed when King Kong hammered at the gates of the city.

Neither was Germany immune from the madness. There people carted wheelbarrows of Deutschmarks in order to buy loaves of bread. Something was seriously wrong here. Surely someone was eating well. Earth hadn't turned into a wasteland . . .

L'Homme Moyen Sensuel

STEFAN AND LIDA talked to the cook while she sliced sorrels and onions and split chicken breasts and melted butter and mixed it with bread crumbs in saucepans the size of bathtubs. Lida even asked the cook to join them upstairs in a *folie à trois*, but the woman, a brunette from Normandy, stared back icily, and Lida never repeated the offer.

While Zenon was busy getting himself shot, Stefan was acquiring wounds of a different sort. He had fallen in with Madame Mathilda Poprovska and her daughter, Lida. They were women of no modest means, and Stefan offered just the kind of diversion they wanted.

Madame Poprovska and he played a game called Catherine the Great, which involved ropes and pulleys, a twelve-inch candle, jodhpurs, a carefully aligned mirror, a riding crop, and whipped cream.

He'd come to Paris a mudman. Formless and eager, he hoped Baudelaire, Delacroix, and the City of Light would help him find himself. Lida, Madame Poprov-ska's daughter, sat in his compartment on the train. Crossing the Alps, St. Bernard (the man, not the dog) was said to have averted his eyes. He did not wish to be distracted from his meditations. Stefan missed the mountains entirely because his were fixed on the gentle slopes and graded cheeks of Lida's face. Later she walked off with his umbrella. When he chased her, she handed it back to him, scalding his wrist with her gloved finger.

At the Gare de L'Est he gaped at funnels of smoke pluming toward the open sky, the writhing scarves, walking sticks, muffs, top hats, and especially the pretty, whitewashed women.

He'd left Austria without finishing his degree. He burned his thesis on the dietary habits of the Desert Fathers before boarding the train.

His interest in the mortifications of saints grew out of his stay in Vienna, where everyone was sex-crazy. In that superior city, people appeared to riot over symphonies and oil paintings. In reality, they fought over sex. The place burned with brilliant lunatics: Schiele, Kokoschka, Mahler, Kraus, Berg, Strauss, Gerstle, Schoenberg. These last two were a pair. First Gerstle screwed Schoenberg's wife, then he made up for it by hanging himself. Schoenberg, cuckolded, hallucinated demonic laughter. This came to be called atonal music. Stefan had seen Kokoschka's play, *Murder, the Hope of Women,* and it shook his simple soul. Not that he knew anything about music, painting, or theater. He hung out in cafés, smoking, brooding, theorizing. He was often in love.

You become on the outside what you yearn for within.

He was the stallion who needed breaking.

She used the candle first.

In 1933 a famine devoured the old country.

The cream was an ointment. He lay naked on his back. She lathered him up.

All the grain the villages produced was shipped to the cities. The farmers were left with nothing.

He let himself be cuffed; let her hoist him above her. He noticed her looking past him at herself in the ceiling mirror.

The NKVD took the children who hung around the train stations, trying to pick up the food that had fallen off during loading, and herded them into an empty car where they were kept like chickens. Fed on single coffee beans and bread crumbs, the children starved to death.

Peaking, she screamed, clawed, ripped pillows, wept. What inspired such operatic orgasms?

In Kirovohrad, the peasants left their unwanted children in the village square. There was no food for them at home. The authorities rounded up the new orphans and led them to Children's Town, miles from the village. The only food the children had was what they could catch and kill with their own hands. They too slowly starved to death. Buried in shallow graves, their bodies were often dragged out of the earth by dogs.

Mathilda refused to relieve him. She left that up to her daughter. He often waited in the pulley for several hours until Lida, his pale Pole from the train, appeared in the doorway. Sometimes she came dressed as Eve. He would be sitting in the chair behind the vanity staring at two pairs of gray eyes blinking like owls above his head. Two smiles, four fingers rubbing the wires in his neck, then one long face leaning forward, sullen breasts pressing his prickly hair, picking up a tube, squeezing cream onto sand-colored fingers which rose and rubbed the temples, massaging the cream into his face, mascara painting rapid lids, then rouge and lipstick. "We're twins," Lida said as they lay in bed for an hour without touching until hands reached for thighs which bloomed open tropically, slower than morning glories, finding the place slick and sticky in one case, and in the other, hard and warm, all night. This was his history, the way lips pressed into a cotton bra, forming itself over the nipple, the beige skin visible in the translucency. His teeth lifting that bra over a breast and a tongue tasting bare skin, the hard polyp covered with bumps, and thumb dropping down to clitoris through the thinner fabric of the panties. A hand settled on the wetness, the venus mound alive and the material easily pushed aside though the fingers abstained from contact with the wet bare flesh, the culmination of these invasions, the last discovery before the immersion. Rising on elbow to fuck with the eyes and then with the tongue, hands milking the breasts and cock drilling, her legs out and high in the air, the body shaped like a Y, the only question, the dark hairs running the rut from cunt to asshole, the smooth unmarked hills on either side into which he tumbled, driving and lapping until she pounded the pillow with the back of her hand, her head whipping side to side, her hair falling over her eyes and her mouth, hand opening and shutting . . .

Stefan always remembered the room: chairs in patterned blue silk, mauve curtains, a rose oriental rug. Chinoiserie, slightly faded. A screen with a peacock painted over the white, semitransparent paper. A hint of Mathilda's incense. And the strangest wallpaper. Three panels, repeated hundreds of times, retold the story of Eve and Adam. In the first, the couple slouch, holding hands, below the notorious tree. Eve's olive-skinned belly pouts above a hairless crotch and Adam's groin glisters like a half-peeled avocado. Whatever erotic spark once surged through them has died. They look grim. About as sexual as two badminton players at a nudist colony. The tree dominates. Its bark is silver, veined with rose. Its branches taper into wrists capped with scowling human faces. The whole is sheathed in a foglike blush. The other panels are murkier: the couple playing the beast with two backs; Eve giving birth to a phoenix. The images were drawn from Mathilda's pet mystic's sacred texts.

For two decades, and more, Stefan lived in a drunken haze. He moved between the Poprovskas' mansion and the homes of several other mistresses, before finally going down to the whorehouse in Marseille. Even when he stayed put, in the Poprovskas' house, he wasn't always sure who was in bed with him. But it was definitely his tongue on a clitoris, the split grape he nibbles with his teeth, almost spitting it out, rubbing the flat of his palm against the open wet mouth till he is so hot he thinks of the one-eyed night clerk in the hotel; and she shouts *oh, oh,* so that he rises to silence her mouth, afraid the servants will hear, and he places his cock back down there and pushes in until she moans, louder and louder; and she starts to spasm, jerking her legs, pressing them against him hard and harder as though trying to break down a door, to get to himself, even now he is still inside himself inside her and then he, no different from anyone, falls asleep. This was the real history.

And during this time, seven million people in the old country were murdered.

In his unfinished history of the world, Stefan wrote that all wars, beginning with the battle of Troy, were about fucking. Not money, or territory, or munitions, or racial supremacy, or nationality. These were secondary causes. He thought of the Chagga tribe, who lived at the foot of the Himalayas and who insisted that the First World War was the outcome of a family feud. It had been prophesied in their sacred books that if one brother killed another, the whole world would be dragged into the struggle. All attempts to fix the causes of war to economics or politics missed the point, and were no different from the speculations of the Himalayan Chagga. No, it was clear to him that when men discovered the limitations of sexual communion, they became convinced they had failed at love. After that, what was there left to lose? Maybe things had not always been like this. Maybe in previous ages human ties had proven durable and sufficiently satisfying. Love, however, had simply not worked out for his generation.

In war, it's our generals we turn to for guidance; in peacetime, it's the genitals that rule.

How rich Rozdorizha seemed to its people, this race of Calibans so mute they could never say what was hurting them or why. They would just as soon torch a house to settle an argument or ride a horse to death to get over their anger because what good did talking ever do? Ill bred, ill clothed, ill traveled — but well fed, because the earth loved them — they thought themselves worldly. They had daily contact with foreigners from strange and devious places. Their town was a crossroad. The world converged around their several thousand fecund acres. Sometimes what drew visitors to this insolent nowhere was wheat, other times coal, and later, oil. The people guarded their land like bees their drowsy queen. They weren't always successful in staving off the entrepreneurs, so they compromised and, for a price, doled out favors.

Shaped and shaded by the east and west and north and south, Rozdorizha changed, grew, contracted, burned, and was rebuilt, burned again, and like the phoenix, reemerged. Just as the city was trimmed and pruned and civilized, so the people, once rude as trees, learned to dress, to shave, to bathe, to read, to buy, to sell, to cheat, to lie. The trees watched the people grow smaller. The moss-covered apples in the Zabobon orchards wondered why the new generation could not reach up to pluck their fruits, why they needed ladders when, in the old days, Toor had used them for stools on which he sat swigging from a skull cup.

Mortal Stakes

In 1942 Zenon Zabobon — sixty, balding, but vigorous — had many Nazi friends.

He worked tirelessly at St. Cyril's Hospital, near the train station, where German officers went to play cards and flirt with the female staff.

Sitting down with a captain, or even a colonel, to a game of chess or *Tarok* (a German version of bridge), he spoke on behalf of some countryman or other who'd gotten himself into trouble with the authorities. The Germans, though aware of his work with the partisans, listened closely. While they had no intention of keeping their promise to establish a free and independent Ukraine, they needed the country as a buffer zone between themselves and Russia. Zenon seemed trustworthy. He said frankly he wished they'd never entered his city. But his contempt was tempered by an unusual pragmatism.

They used him to keep track of his people. "Who is cutting our phone lines?" Captain Reichman asked. Or: "Who is leaving barrels of dead fish outside the police station?"

Zenon never told them. But they could rest assured

that from then on the telephone lines would be left alone, and the deliveries of fish would stop.

He arrived at the hospital every afternoon around three-thirty. The men sat down before the chess board, Zenon smoking his pipe or chewing on the earpiece of his bifocals, Reichman dragging deep on a Lucky Strike, punctuating sentences with a phlegmy cough.

"You should have an examination," Zenon suggested.

"My asthma. Very bad when I was a boy. And the city air . . . "

"I know."

"You don't mean to leave the bishop there, do you?" Cough.

When Zenon needed to raise a delicate matter, he intensified his game. Fear of losing kept his opponent off balance.

"I understand you're holding Rudenko."

"The arsonist?"

"That story's fabricated by the Russians . . . "

"You don't say?"

"Alas . . . "

"I'll look into it. You know how counterproductive disinformation is."

Zenon answered in English, "Quite."

His other reason for cultivating the Germans was because he was hiding Jews in his apartment. There were five of them: his former colleague Eddie Glick and his family.

Late one night, several months after the Germans arrived, Zenon answered a knock on the door. He found himself staring into Eddie Glick's dark eyes. His face appeared smeared with charcoal. "The Germans go to the ghetto every night. Every night they arrest people. Sometimes they shoot them right there," Eddie said.

"I know," said Zenon. "Where's the family?"

Eddie's wife and three children were waiting downstairs under the stairwell for the results of the interview.

After they were safely inside, Eddie told Zenon and Natalka how they had snuck aboard a wagon of corpses being hauled out of the ghetto and slipped off at an appropriate moment.

Everyone stayed up the rest of the night hammering together a false wall in the pantry behind which the five Glicks hid and, in a manner of speaking, lived. Their tiny quarters reminded Lastivka of a mausoleum.

Lastivka was home now much of the time. The Germans had finally closed the university, where she'd studied acting. She was months short of receiving her diploma. Bored, she put on shows for her family: she tap danced, imitated Edith Piaf and Marlene Dietrich. She previewed her upcoming role with an underground theater troupe as Ophelia. The five Glicks applauded with gusto.

"I regret I won't be there to throw roses," Eddie said.

Fact: the Germans had spotted the Glicks entering the building.

"Give them their Jews," Reichman said, coughing. "What are five more or less to us? Zenon is more important than that."

A third reason Zenon fraternized with the occupying forces was that he was having an affair with Captain Reichman's wife.

A snow queen from the Rhineland, with high cheeks, flat blue eyes, and heavy blonde hair coiled in a chain on top of her head, Elizabeth's direct manner, much like her husband's, scared most of the men she met, and she was lonely as only the most beautiful women are. In her presence men either turned idiot (Your . . . eyes . . . lips . . . those buttons . . .), or they assumed someone as fine as that was hitched to Ivan the Terrible.

Zenon had met her at a session of the Near-Death Society.

After the meeting he walked her home and was invited up for a schnapps. The apartment once belonged to the editor for whom he'd written the article on Scythian pottery for which he had been arrested nearly thirty years before. It thrilled him to sit there with his enemy. Elizabeth, who spoke perfect Ukrainian, played Liszt on the Victrola. A crystal ball sat on the coffee table. The couple huddled over it.

"I see doves," she whispered.

At Near-Death Society meetings they often discussed the end of the war, the arrival of a permanent peace.

They established a routine: after playing chess with her husband, the captain, Zenon would wait long enough for the officer to get back to the station house. Then he would hurry to his Elizabeth.

Risk gave the moment life. And he needed a place where he could deposit his hopes and his dreams without fear of forfeiting the capital.

One afternoon over chess, Captain Reichman said, "The order's come down. If you don't send them away tonight, you'll all be arrested."

Zenon, poised to castle, moved his bishop instead. Dumb. Reichman's knight had a fork. "Why now?"

"Not much more I can tell you. After the war, we'll talk."

Water Remembers, Or:
The Dead Return as Butterflies

THAT EVENING, after arranging for the Glicks' escape, Zenon gave Natalka three tickets to Klagenfurt in Austria. "Train leaves at eleven. Hurry."

He convinced Stefan, who'd been idling around the city for several months, smoking in cafés, making notes in his journal, to go with them.

Before Zenon escorted the Glicks to the car that was to take them, in time, to Switzerland, Eddie came up to Stefan, who was smoking a cigarette, staring gloomily into his empty black bag. Eddie smiled. "Who knows?" he said. "Who knows? This might be of some use to you later." He handed Stefan an envelope.

"Good luck to you," Stefan said.

"May we meet again. In a better place."

"Eddie, we'll be back home before you can say *kreplach*."

"This isn't our home, Stefan."

Stefan slipped the envelope into his pocket without giving it a second thought.

Stefan hardly noticed the war. He'd arrived late one night at his brother's residence and asked if he might stay for a bit, in the living room.

"Aren't you going in the wrong direction?" Zenon asked with some surprise. He hadn't seen his brother in years.

Stefan shrugged. "This is home." He said nothing about where he'd been. Some claimed he'd been wounded while working with the French resistance. Others suggested he'd contracted syphilis. Except for the goatee, he'd shorn his roguishness. He'd grown so thin, his arms and legs seemed like props for the gray cotton suit that billowed about him. He limped (it seemed he'd developed a clubfoot) from café to café, scribbling in his notebooks and smoking cigarettes.

Reluctantly, he agreed to chaperone his sister-in-law and niece to Austria. Afterward, he intended to return to Rozdorizha. His family had lived there a thousand years, suffering attacks by Turks, Tartars, Poles, and Russians. The city would survive the Germans.

The train moved slowly.

"Water remembers," he said to his neice.

"What, Uncle?" Lastivka looked at this stranger, with his monocle and his dolphin-handled cane.

Mountains and fields rolled past his window. He dragged on his cigarette and brooded. "That's what the scientists say. They say that if you take two glasses and fill one with boiling water and another with tap water and then you wait for the one that's been boiled to cool down until it's exactly the same temperature as the tap water, and then you put them both in the freezer, the tap water will freeze first because the molecules inside the other glass will remember that they had recently been boiled. They won't change their state willingly. Think of it."

Lastivka looked at the trees. Isn't that nice, she thought, we've been handed over to a madman.

Lastivka was not depressed. On the contrary. She felt the large world starting to open before her. She had waited for this journey her whole life. They'd lived with danger so long, and had, so far, successfully negotiated their world. Lastivka did not worry about her father. God would take care of him. He would follow them in a day or two. She'd meet the friends she left behind when the war ended, which was bound to be soon. The confidence of youth, which knows that it can never die, lifted her into a bright sphere. Hope was everywhere.

She looked tenderly at her mother, who slept with her head back against the seat, her mouth open. Her cheeks were thin — the rations in the last months had been meager. Not even Jadviga, who'd stayed behind, had been able to find meat on the black market. She would miss Jadviga, the cook. But her mother was here, and she felt safe. The two of them had survived so much already, and their friendship was one of her life's delights.

Stefan, at sixty, saw it differently.

In the sixteenth century an ancestor had been knighted by Poland's grand duke before he was hanged for negotiating with the Cossacks. His great-great-great-grandfather spat in Napoleon's face when asked for the keys to the city treasury. For which he was shot. It was the city in which Halka, Jadviga's niece, slipped into his bed one night when he was thirteen and persuaded him his plans for becoming a priest were perverse. It was to

Rozdorizha he fled after Marseille and the Poprovska affair.

In Rozdorizha he could sleep. Rozdorizha was home: every sliver of granite had been touched by the hands or the glances of the Zabobons. He felt as much a part of the place as the rivers who, seeing him ride by, murmured sadly. He reassured them: as soon as he delivered the girls, he would return to his delicious, aimless, peripatetic existence, lounging in cafés and scratching notes toward his *Theory of Marriage* and *The History of Rozdorizha and the World.*

The grass bent in sorrow. *Don't go,* cried the leaves. *Don't leave,* groaned the stones.

Go, boomed Toor. *Fast as you can.*

Later, after Lastivka was asleep, Stefan was fishing in his pocket for a match when he came upon the envelope Eddie had handed him. He opened it. Inside was a pocket handkerchief. He shook it out. Something dropped to the floor. Stefan bent down, picked it up. It was a diamond. A bread crumb, leading them home.

An Expense of Spirit

ZENON STAYED behind. He said he had financial matters to settle. In fact, he wanted a final evening with Elizabeth.

It was his sole indiscretion. He told himself Elizabeth might be useful to the Ukrainian cause. That it was Natalka's fault for pushing him away. That he loved the captain's wife. But a voice, which began speaking to him while he lay beside the corpses in Chlib, insisted he craved Elizabeth's breasts, and nothing more.

Unfortunately, Captain Reichman returned early and saw Zenon leave the apartment.

The next day he was arrested.

At an informal hearing, Colonel Stiller, Captain Reichman's superior, a large-boned man with thick pink lips whom Zenon beat regularly at *Tarok*, and who as a result respected this gifted intellectual, said, "I could have you shot. Not for what you've done to Reichman. He's not seriously injured. He'll survive. A little humiliation is healthy for an ambitious young man. Makes him a realist. Yes, I know why he had you arrested. Moreover, I know Frau Reichman. If anyone's to blame, it's nature.

"It's the Jews in the pantry that trouble me."

The direct line. A surprise. Zenon groped in his pocket for his pipe. Not there. Impossible. He'd never forgotten it before. Bad sign. "You've known about them all along."

"We hoped their stay was temporary. And that you'd be discreet. Instead, singing nightly. Yiddish songs! Craziness."

Zenon studied the boiled egg on the colonel's desk. Was it a late breakfast? Early lunch? They wanted something from him; they could have arrested him anytime. The egg sat unshelled and ungarnished in a plain wooden cup. His left hand plucked at an earlobe. That voice, like the half-remembered words of parental counsel, reminded him he was bound by the rules of the Near-Death Society to behave toward the world with infinite gentleness, and *no exceptions!* Moreover, he felt guilty. He deserved punishment.

"So, Herr Professor," Stiller said. "Always, in life, two choices." Then, being a reflective man, added: "Give or take a few. In any case. The firing squad. Or, my alternative. Become one of us. I don't mean a spy. I invite you to accept German citizenship. Indeed, I urge you to. We'll make no awkward demands. It will be a symbolic gesture. Good faith on both sides, eh?"

Zenon thought of the wax people, the collaborators, those bitter men and women who worked with the Nazis to get revenge on people they believed had wronged them. In the last years he'd seen terrible things. Boys with nails driven through their eyes. Grenades stuffed into women's vaginas, the pins pulled. And so on.

He thought of Elizabeth. And Natalka. The natural generosity of women.

"I'm sorry, Colonel. Truth is, you're a lousy card player. As for me, I'm closer to the grave than to Germany."

The lines sounded theatrical. He blushed. Posing, he thought to himself. People never stop posing.

The colonel took the old man at his word, and the next morning Zenon Zabobon became a citizen of that least exclusive yet infinitely august and oldest of republics.

Less than a month later, the Germans were gone, driven out by the Soviet army.

———

The Armenian church in Klagenfurt was named for St. Gregory the Enlightener. His story was told in vivid icons on the walls.

Before he could convert King Tiridates to the one true faith, Gregory was put through twelve torments. He was strung from a tree by his toes. Every hair on his head was burned off. A hot iron was shoved in his ear, and so on. Natalka sought solace in the company of the icons. She understood the pain reflected in them. No longer the eager girl who fled the village hoping to play the piano in the concert halls of Europe, she glared at the grizzly paintings on the walls. What were arrows in flesh beside a broken heart? What was a crown of thorns in the light of her loss? She'd gladly wear one if it meant she could have her husband back. She and Zenon had been one body. He was her life, her sanity, her home.

She cursed every saint in the church. Then she cursed the Germans and the Jews both. No more, she thought, she could take no more. From now on she'd live in retrospect. In a world where Zenon still breathed, where he walked up and down the room lecturing her on nationalism, the women's movement, the wisdom of Marx, the role of the peasant. A world where they were both young and future-laden. Nothing more from the outside world would ever enter. She was at last complete.

I understand, sighed Toor, who'd never forgotten the wife he'd lost to War.

Vienna, Capital of the World

To a man wanting a swim in a quiet, lily-festooned pond, Vienna is no paradise, not even in peacetime, never mind in 1945. Stefan settled for soaks in the communal bathtub under the stairwell on the second floor of the rooming house. He watched the gnarled ankles of Mrs. Stern, the blunt boots of Ivan Starosolsky, the slippers of Eva Lozynsky skittering down the hall in hopes of rubbing up against Vladimir Kozak's weathered work boots.

This was not the Vienna in which he'd wasted his youth. The place was soulless. Freud, Musil, Roth: long gone. Max Reinhardt was in Hollywood. The Opera House and St. Stephen's Cathedral looked like Stonehenge. Russians approached the city in which the Rothschilds and their set once played Marie Antoinette.

Not that Stefan felt much sympathy for the *Hofburgers*. It pleased him to imagine Napoleon at Schönbrunn. In 1916 Vienna had radiated calm. Like all centers of empire, it worked hard to preserve a façade of normalcy, no matter the cost to sanity. It behaved as though it had nothing to do with the war it had begun. Murder, mustard gas, trenches — what were these to the city of joys? Nineteen sixteen had been the Year of the Waltz. That fall premiered operettas by Beratsky, Eysler, Fall, Jarno, Stolz.

All history now. No minuets or poignant lieder sounded from the concert halls. Nevermore. They'd been excrescences of the moment, the short-lived blooms of power. Henceforth its art would feel like dried flowers.

He turned the pages in his book, its sheets curling from moisture: *Growing civilizations do not perish from the pangs of one autumn; they merely shed their leaves. Inertia is the only mortal danger. The poet is he who breaks for us the bonds of habit.*

Wise to stay off the streets where lunatics danced out the psychoses of defeat. On Bergerstrasse an old man peeled off his clothes, shouting verses from Jeremiah at bewildered passersby. No. No one was bewildered now. In six years people had seen everything. Man is wolf to man. There's no such thing as *humanity*. Only individuals who attain that status.

And why did the nations so furiously rage? He thought of the failed Dreikaiserbund, the terrible problems with the Russians in the Balkans, those Obrenovic kings of Serbia, the invincible sultan of Turkey, the trigger-happy Serbs losing their lives over Bosnia-Herzegovina. Professor Heinrich Friedjung, the radical incendiary (or vice versa) condemning the Belgrade revolutionaries. Or the Hapsburg minister of foreign affairs, who'd replaced Ashrental in 1912, and who believed the Ukrainian question was key because what they did affected both the Russians and the Austrians. The Austrians wanted to make sure Ukrainians developed their sense of identity and weren't Russified, in this way keeping them loyal to the emperor rather than the czar. The minister wrote to the Austrian premier: "I say that our relations with Russia, which are of such great importance, will depend in the future on our success in preventing the Russification of the Ukrainians, which is being vigorously pursued on our territory, and in preserving the separate character of this nation, and by raising its civilization." That had been in June 1914, while Stefan was in Paris with the Poprovskas, mother *and* daughter, and his brother was falling in love with Natalka.

So much history. And how was it possible that the really important things happened only to others?

In the streets people cried that the kingdom of God was near, but Stefan knew it was the Kingdom of America around the corner. Kingdom of Washington, New York, Detroit.

Maybe places, like feelings, faded. Maybe cities bloomed just once, and the rest was a long withering. There was no glory in the past. Glory was a present-tense affair. A man's work was to find a way to add his solitary flame to the general conflagration.

While Vienna greeted the Russians, Stefan read: *And perhaps the day does not pass but a man may burn with desire for a woman and for her daughter.*

The building trembled. Water splashed from the tub. The bombs neared.

From Paris to this tepid tub. Men never understood that words they said today determined where they'd be tomorrow. We are so horribly free.

Silence. How pleasant. After a decade syncopated by gunfire, acres of silence might cure him.

He heard the souls breathing in the shelter sixty feet below. And a mouse mapping the inside of the wall. What did the mice make of the war?

Another flake of plaster fell, and another. A snow-storm. His mother's house at Christmas. His dead brothers. Had he really believed he'd return to Roz-dorizha? He had promised to take care of Natalka and Lastivka.

Snow, snow.

. . . *one law of harmony governs the whole world of things* . . .

He'd met the author at a dinner at Mathilda's, along with Rouault, Apollinaire, and a few others who'd since made names for themselves.

Somehow the mouse turned out to be a bomb. The room exploded.

Natalka levered the opener. The can sighed. Stefan opened his eyes on the sight of Nurse Schmidt staring tenderly at a thermometer. She seemed to read it like a love letter. He listened. No explosions. No grinding of tanks. Natalka offered him a slice of canned peach. He tried focusing on the glistening crescent, but his eyes strayed after Schmidt.

"You look happy," Stefan observed.

"The Germans are gone."

"Finally. Now let's get to the American sector."

Natalka swallowed while a man in the neighboring bed cried out, "Watch out for Kaganovich!"

The streets were dangerous. The Russians were in —

discriminate, favoring neither blondes nor redheads nor brunettes.

After he left the hospital, Stefan began politicking, making connections, reasserting personal gifts long dormant. First he took the *brilliant* Eddie gave him and sold it to a one-armed man he met in a café. Then he used the cash to buy a suitcase of cigarettes and several bottles of whiskey. These were the drugs that opened doors.

The commander of the Russian regiment stationed near their district was a Ukrainian who protected his folk, slipping them extra ration coupons and escorting Miss Pretty Lastivka to the park, where oaks shadowed lilies in the summer sun as though the war had never happened. The two chatted, walking the imperious boulevards. But, though forsythia and lilac semaphored the blood and the commander was clearly interested, Lastivka stayed in the cocoon she'd spun to save herself from the noise of battle. She felt that at best she would soon begin to feel again. But not yet. Everything was still too unsettled. They learned they were leaving the following week for the displaced persons camp set up by the Americans in Berchtesgaden.

The International Relief Organization

THE WAR was over. Millions of people, their homes destroyed, their countries dismembered, their dead abandoned, found themselves freer than they'd ever hoped to be. The Allies learned again that winning a war was half the battle. Now they faced the consequences of their actions. Every bomb dropped—by either side—created new problems. The victims did not just disappear. Had the Allies turned their backs on the vanquished, they would have created whole populations that lived in a state of permanent rebellion. Instead, the winners chose, humanely and wisely, to repair the damage.

Displaced persons camps were established throughout Germany and Austria. People poured into them by the millions. Run by the Allies, the camps quickly came to resemble independent nation-states. Wise Rome knew when to sit back and let people take care of themselves.

Camp Orlik, set up for Ukrainians, was located at the foot of Mt. Watzman, in Berchtesgaden, not far from the mountain where Hitler had maintained his Eagle's Nest hideaway.

Camp life was social and spirited. Two thousand people lived in the brick and concrete dormitories of what had formerly been army barracks. Families of four or more had their own room, each equipped with a Primus propane stove and electric lights. After six years of war no one really minded the close quarters. No grenades, few informants. What luxury!

The people quickly organized a high school, an art school, a vocational school. The most popular subject of course was English. Knowledge was power. The local government needed a liaison with the camp authorities, who were Americans.

The Ukrainians also set up their own hospital and police force. There was a cafeteria. There was a theater in which people watched Humphrey Bogart and Ingrid Bergman in *Casablanca*.

So these were the Americans, Lastivka thought, her eyes tearing. These are our new masters.

In the camp she saw her first black man, a soldier who managed to secure for her one of the coveted torn parachutes out of which the women made dresses. They dyed it, laced it with mosquito netting and *voilà!* Party time.

In Berchtesgaden Lastivka resumed piano lessons. "See," Natalka grumbled. "I told you one day you'd run to it."

Her instructor, Meister Rakovsky, a short, shrill man, red ascot wrapping his neck, raked back his fluted

white hair with wirey fingers while scolding his talent-
less disciples. Lessons were held in the supply warehouse. Worried students shuffled past tins of milk, tuna,
tomatoes, all bearing the stamp and promise of efficient,
matter-mastering America. They were expected to
bring their own light bulbs. Each entered the little
room, climbed a crate, screwed in his or her bulb,
suffered a half-hour—because not one had the whisper
of a gift—unscrewed the bulb, and made room for
Rakovsky's next victim. Meister Rakovsky used the moment of darkness to probe his nose. If his pupil chanced
to be a pretty girl, he tried fondling—a buttock, a
breast, a boot, it didn't matter.

The students kept coming. Everyone had time. The
sourest spirits suddenly felt musical. Music might translate their tangled feelings, the losses, the things they'd
seen. Music lessons nurtured the fiction of normalcy
they needed to combat the inevitable strains of camp life.

People experimented with alternate selves. Many
had passed their teenage years running—what could
they know of who they were? Now they would see, dis-
cover, redraw. Plumbers studied French; philosophers
looked into plumbing. The piano was the perfect play-
ground. Septuagenarians lusted for their half-hour of
dusting ivory.

Greasy Rakovsky, convicted by his own genius, grew
rich.

———

Certain she was alone, Lastivka lit a cigarette. Every
few minutes she squeezed her straw bag for the bulb.

"Early?"

She turned: a black beret, a trenchcoat (but it was sunny outside). Something familiar in the voice, the hint of a growl.

"My lesson's at three. As always."

"Ah, no, dear." Blue eyes, faintly Asian, suggested Tartar blood. His features were fine as a Roman's.

She ran a finger through her hair. "Wrong. That's my time."

He spoke with a swagger.

"My lesson's always at three," she said.

"I talked to Rakovsky this morning. He said three," the stranger pressed.

"Must have slipped." Then added, her voice falling, "Drinks, you know."

"What's your piece?"

"Rachmaninoff's Prelude. An amazing . . . " She forgot her annoyance. Her new interest in the music inspired her. She opened the score and showed him the part that was giving her trouble. "See?"

He laughed. "Where are you going?"

"Not up to me. Uncle will decide. And you?"

"America. Mad Yankees. Baseball team, you know."

"You have opinions." She was flirting. What was his name? Secret thoughts he could easily read raced through her mind.

"It's the new Austro-Hungarian Empire. The new Rome. Power shifts, you know. Money moves."

He buttoned his coat. She squeezed her bulb and stared down. The door opened. A bespeckled girl with stringy braids stepped out. She clutched a sheaf of music in her left hand while the right closed over the top buttons of her pale blue sweater.

"Miss Zabobon . . . "

Meister Rakovsky's voice, high and tonic.

Arkady smiled, clicked his heels, and prodded the door.

The room smelled of sweet American after-shave.

"I'll be right here," Arkady said.

"I take care of myself," she replied.

Inside, she rushed to the piano, kicking the treacherous crate out of her way, climbed the stool, and screwed in the bulb. When the light came on, she found her teacher sitting on the crate staring at her legs. She jumped down, brushed and adjusted the stool.

Rakovsky was in a foul mood. He kept pinching his nose while glancing off into the corner.

He hummed.

Lines of sweat covered her brow with unscored staves.

The pedal slipped under her worn sole.

Rakovsky hummed louder.

Tears veiled her eyes but she drove on. Then she hit a wrong note.

"Legato, legato. Fool. Listen. This is how Horowitz might do it . . . "

The piano changed him. The man showed a grasp of the theorems limning the heart's buried trills. Harder, deeper: he was inside the notes, breathing out, swinging with Terpsichore on a rope above the abyss. Lastivka held her breath. He stopped suddenly, stood up, and resumed his familiar role.

The light seemed to wink as the bulb flared and died.

She felt a hand on her thigh and she leaped up, knocking over the stool. "Oh . . . " The door opened. Arkady stood there grinning. He offered her his bulb like a bouquet of flowers.

"Slava Lastivka Zabobon? Arkady Vorog."

"You're early," snapped Rakovsky.

"No, it's all right, my time is up," Lastivka said.

"No, no. Lida Gruda is waiting to give me my English lesson," Arkady said.

"I thought you said three," she persisted.

"Three-thirty."

"Very kind. But no. Think of Broadway," said Lastivka.

"I'll settle for Harlem."

"Where?" she asked.

He turned to Rakovsky. "Three-thirty tomorrow, sir?"

The old man waved his iron claw. "Four!"

"The light bulb," Lastivka said.

"I'll get it tonight."

"You don't know where I live," she said.

"Yes, I do," he nodded.

Rich Rakovsky inherited another bulb.

———

It was already dark. Not a star to be seen through the clouds. Lastivka and Arkady sat in a park in Berchtesgaden itself. The camp had begun to feel too small for their dreams.

She wanted to know all about him. For the first time in his life, Arkady spoke openly to a woman.

His father had been a farmer before becoming a *kulak* and getting himself shot.

For centuries the Vorogs worked the land two hundred *versts* southeast of Kiev. Arkady hated it. The boring eternal sky depressed a man: to think of all that world below you'd never see! And the natives, their talk confined to women and crops and God; and the women themselves, either coy or cautious, or too wild, fierce as ferrets, with dark skin and hips wide like troughs and foreheads narrow as teaspoons. He hated his routine, rising early, tweaking cows, scattering chicken feed, and scything grass, though his father bought a tractor as soon as he could. Luckily, his father sympathized, because he'd been to Vienna once and heard the great tenor Björling sing *Turandot*. He never forgot that night. In his mind he traveled often to the city of top hats and long coats and gray kid gloves, the land of blown-glass swans and paper machier crèches and earrings shaped like zeppelins where, the old man mused while burying his arm to the elbow in manure, a man could happily waste a lifetime, which was hardly any time at all. There were good reasons for wanting to move to the city. But a man had obligations.

One day Arkady and his mother were returning home from their annual pilgrimage to Rovno, where his mother's sister lived.

In his hand the ten-year-old held a wooden horse an uncle had whittled for him.

He watched his mother staring at the tracks, smoking her pipe. Minutes before, the cicadas had fallen silent. The birds had disappeared. The boy heard footsteps below. He looked again at his mother puffing her pipe.

This was around '31. The Bolsheviks had arrived.

His mother whispered, "Come here, boy."

He felt her fear. To him, all of it, including the shooting he heard whenever he visited town, belonged to the vague and anxious world of grown-ups, for which he had no use.

He squatted at her feet. She was wearing her husband's old brown leather army boots with the metal eyelets.

Four soldiers appeared at the head of the stairs. One was so fat the boy wanted to laugh. Their uniforms were ribboned with mud. Arkady had read that Napoleon once slapped a corporal because the brass button of an epaulet wasn't shiny enough.

"What's this? A woman of substance."

His mother sucked her pipe.

"A walking mattress."

"Wouldn't want to sleep on it."

Arkady glared.

A soldier leaned over and yanked the wooden horse from the child. "Want to see how we break wild horses?"

"Leave him," said his mother.

"Oh, the mattress speaks."

She closed her hands over her pipe. Smoke escaped from between her fingers.

The men passed a bottle, wiping their mouths on green coats.

"What about the mattress?"

"You want water, mattress?" The soldier offered the bottle. She slapped it out of his hands and it broke, scattering diamonds.

"Wonder if the mattress squeaks."

74

Arkady could never forgot the scene that followed.

His mother resisted. Someone crushed the pipe. Boots danced in the air. There was laughter, a little rain from clouds fleeing the mountains. That was nothing. One soldier held the boy's arms and legs, and he watched and felt something astonishing happen inside him.

The sun was beginning to rise above Mt. Watzman when he told Lastivka, who sat very near him, that in that moment he realized life was a game. Somehow he concluded: that there was a God, no one could control the way things turned out, and there was nothing to fear. He never strayed from these three hunches.

Then his father was shot.

"What happened to your mother?" she asked.

"I don't know," he said. "After Father was killed, we moved north to my uncle's. I went to school in the city. She wrote me letters each month. One month they stopped. Then I had to leave."

He spoke calmly. It was essential for him to keep his mind locked on the future. He was a man with a mission and *now* was a doorway. He wasn't sure where he was going, but he knew he'd keep moving, harnessed, always looking ahead.

Lastivka stayed silent a while. "Do you want to look for her?"

"What for?"

He slid his arm over her shoulder. Encouraged by her stillness, he pulled her closer. She said nothing.

The sun slowly ladled out its light.

Lastivka was in love.

She thought of everything that had happened over

the last years. Millions had died; countries had disappeared. None of it mattered as much as their meeting.

Arkady was more calculating. He'd been with many women. The physical connection always satisfied him. Here there were other considerations, questions of character which couldn't be answered in a night. Would she be a good woman? His feelings strayed like clouds: there were days of dumb gazing when he felt nothing and others when, standing near her, he was glazed with light, as though he were moving in a dimension once removed from his usual haunts.

———

In 1950 Stefan approved the marriage of Lastivka and Arkady.

It amused him to be consulted. He thought of himself as the consort of ladies of the night, a lover of the wrong sort of women. But baldness, it seemed, brought respectability unbidden. And as to marriage! If pressed, Stefan would have said men and women were like Cain and Abel to each other: one wandered, the other stayed rooted. They were spirits at odds, and each day they changed parts and slew each other. Every night they were resurrected through the ritual of lovemaking. He'd warned his brother about the business, and look what had happened to him.

Natalka complained that Arkady, now assistant to the commandant, was an upstart, a climber from the backwoods (he was from a village twice the size of the one in which she was raised). Why should he spoil the impeccable genealogy of the Zabobons? The link went back to King Toor in the tenth century. Her daughter merited royalty, or at least a medical doctor. Another insult to live with. But she would not fight with her daughter. She spoke her mind, then retreated, staying true to the vow she made in that Armenian church in Klagenfurt. Life was never going to get *her* hopes up again. While Stefan founded it harder and harder to sleep, Natalka was practically narcoleptic, awake only for meals. She kept dreaming of her mother boiling poppy seeds in a black kettle and her father lashing her brothers with a leather strap, of her sisters bathing in a trough in sunlight surrounded by feeding pigs. Sometimes she saw Toor, naked, his penis plowing the earth. She wished she'd listened more closely to Zenon's stories about this great ancestor.

Stefan liked Arkady. He saw a durable fire in the peasant's eyes: his was just the blood needed to kindle first life in the not-so-new world. Scuttled pseudo-aristocrats like himself stood no chance in America, and he looked forward to a life requited by chess, philosophy, and cigars. He did not mind. He knew Nietzsche was right when he said that anything that doesn't kill you makes you stronger.

"Besides, she's thirty-four."

The wedding was held in a wooden seventeenth-century church nestled between a wine shop and a doctor's office. After the ceremony the party spilled down to the tables by the river. A *bandurist* and a small orchestra sat on a low platform near the water, tuning their instruments.

The sun was out, the sky clear and frivolous as the canopy of a circus tent. Stefan, standing in the doorway of the church, calmly observed the return of innocence and laughter. It would not last, he thought. Not innocence, not laughter. Neither would the misery and gloom certain to follow. Twenty years from now, this wretched, lovely place would be haunted by tourists eager to palm a piece of the spot from which the eagle fell to gouge at Prometheus. *Sic transit . . .*

And, just as Stefan suspected, it was America, Kingdom of the Puritan God, that awaited. Life would be less violent. There would be no land mines or bombs. But they would bring with them the attitudes of people accustomed to defeat. The faithless would fail, and quickly. Freedom was nearly as threatening as its opposite. They would have to be cautious, learn slowly, learn silence. "Don't worry," Arkady reassured him. "It's only temporary. Only until the Americans get the Russians out." That wasn't what Stefan expected, but he said nothing.

Shortly after the wedding, the Zabobon-Vorogs, along with several hundred other denizens of the camp who had finally received the invitations and job offers they needed, traveled by train to Bremen. The International Relief Organization put them up in port hotels for two weeks. Then they boarded the navy transport that was to take them to America.

Passengers, outnumbering beds three to one, slept in

steerage holds. As they were segregated by sex, a favorite occupation of the husbands, wives, and new acquaintances was looking for nooks in which to make love. Sighs and moans emanated from under the stairs, from linen closets.

They were all assigned chores: some worked as tailors, others helped in the kitchen. Arkady was given a mop. They recreated all the organizations they'd had in the camps. They put out a daily paper, filled with gossip and advice about the coming new life, which, they were slowly beginning to understand, would not be the one they had imagined for themselves.

One evening, Lastivka strolled alone on deck. She reached furtively into her pocket and pulled out a cigarette. Arkady disapproved of her smoking but she saw herself as something of a bohemian. She had, after all, once performed as Ophelia. A reviewer for an underground paper described her as mousy. Which she was not. Her eyes were small and darting. But her speech was slow and dreamy, and her voice was low like her father's.

Orange embers danced over the water. The breeze combed back her hair. A sailor, head bowed, walked past, and she dangled the cigarette over the side of the ship. But he was in a hurry, collar up, teeth chattering, and hardly saw her. She herself wasn't cold: prospects and dreams, those feather comforters of the young, kept her from feeling the ice of the air. The ocean, sly vendor of romance, helped by the moon, flashed and lit its various wares; a goose dropped to the deck — then, as if discovering she'd made a wrong turn somewhere, cast forward her snowy neck, pushed up with her feet, and departed. A far ship hooted like an owl. Perhaps it was a cruise boat, chauffeuring the rich, who traveled not because they needed to, but for the sheer pleasure of motion. Ah, the rich. When the apocalypse came, and Lastivka believed it long overdue, the rich alone would get gate passes from St. Peter. Who else could afford their beautiful purity of motive and manner? They were like snails, those creatures favored by God, who had their homes permanently strapped to their backs, making them free and unfettered citizens of the world. "Money is the petrol of life," Arkady told her. He'd read it in a book. A philosophical book. How fortunate she was to have him. He fathomed the world's mechanism like a watchmaker a timepiece.

On the starboard side, a crew of dolphins broke through the waves.

Someone tugged at the hem of her skirt. She looked down. A woman wearing a black babushka snuggled against the wall, sucking a pipe. She was wrapped to the neck in a green army blanket. Stolen, no doubt, from the DP camp. Lastivka owned one just like it. The old woman's feet protruded from the cocoon, showing shoes that wear had frayed into sandals. Her fingers stabbed out at Lastivka, and a phlegmy voice rose from the smoke like a malicious flame, "You will all suffer horribly. You've forgotten your ghosts."

Lastivka crossed herself and hurried away.

When she repeated the prophecy to her new husband, Arkady spat, stuck a toothpick in his mouth, and said, "*Variatka! Durna Baba!* Precisely the type of hot tip I won't miss not getting in America. Americans, thank God, are sane. They have technology!"

Arkady sat near the latrine, whittling a wooden bear. At his feet lay a menagerie: a cossack on horseback (you could see its fetlocks), a girl carrying a bucket, and a *bandura* with sixty-four strings. He'd learned the craft from his uncle. It was sweet to make things. And he sold a few to sailors. Preparing for America.

A man's starting point in life was the luck of the draw. Everything after that happened in reaction to that first accident. Man worked, married, fought, responding to pressures from outside. In America he'd need all his strength. He'd be starting from scratch. He'd feel like a failure.

He prepared for the insults and fixed his gaze on the future. He imagined himself a cowboy in a novel by Karl May, sent to scout the new territory. The hills of the future breathed mystery; there might be gold in the river.

The gold itself wasn't important. He believed in only one thing: the nation. Shaped by the spirit of opposition, he wouldn't rest until his enemies were defeated.

Time to find the guy who ran the black market.

The priest followed Stefan everywhere. He sat beside him at meals; appeared nearby when he walked on deck. He was always smiling, muttering something that sounded like *God's will,* but may have been *Go to hell.*

Stefan was counting gulls, hoping it would make him sleepy, when Father Ivan sidled up.

"Father, Father. I'm not ready for last rites yet. What business is there between us?"

"You remind me of someone."

"The devil?"

"A man from home. Someone I could talk to. He's been dead for years." The priest's face was deely pocked and there was a pimple or chancre near the corner of his mouth.

"How can I help, Father? Nobody I know has dollars."

"No, no. Too late for that. It's peace of mind. But I'll never get it. I've kissed the devil and it's left a tattoo." He pointed to the pimple.

"A pimple, Father? What can you hope for at your age?"

"It's a pineapple . . . "

"It's big, Father."

"Syphilis," the priest confided.

"There are remedies."

"No, I won't take medicine. It cleanses the symptoms without scourging the source."

"Who do I remind you of?"

"Vlodyk. A priest in Rozdorizha."

Stefan expected it.

"Why would you want him?"

"He's dead. Of the same disease. They say he made peace with it."

He was talking about Stefan's father.

"Good-bye," the priest said, slipping into the darkness.

Stefan never saw him again.

Most nights on board the men played cards and discussed places to settle. They were too poor to gamble, so they bet future fortunes: dream dollars, dream houses, dream cars. Business partnerships were formed. Three bricklayers incorporated, and twenty years later a town in Idaho was named Promin in honor of their company.

Arkady sat on a crate, aloof from the group. He liked gambling but was unlucky and forced himself to remain an observer. He discouraged casual conversation. Over the years he'd learned ways for keeping people at bay. Among other things, he was big. In the arms, the thighs, the head. Stefan once described him as being *grande come un cavallo! forte come un lione!* He enjoyed making the bulk and power apparent. Though he seemed to be sitting at ease, arms cupping the back of his head, the inflection of his legs hinted he was crouched and ready to spring; and while he smiled often, particularly at women, there was something about the half-lidded blue eyes and tense gnarled neck that suggested the smile could readily change to a snarl.

Work, they said, was easiest to get in the East. But life was much more civilized in the West. That Pacific climate, Stefan concluded after reading several issues of *Life,* had spawned a rhythm and style unknown to the world since fourteenth-century Provence. The thought of France, the memory of those blonde, thick-lipped odalisques, roiled the blood. He was tempted to test his rhetorical skills and plead a case for the West. But after many nights of listening to his fellow passengers, Arkady decided on New York. There followed a quarrel between husband and wife. Lastivka, forgetting her love of cafés and museums, refused to live without a garden. She had heard New York was entirely concrete and steel.

"It's all temporary. We'll be going home in a few years," Arkady pointed out.

Natalka didn't care. She said she would just as gladly go to Australia. Her indifference enraged Arkady. He glared at her, biting down on his toothpick. Natalka busied herself with her embroidery. She was working on a shirt for the grandson she expected. She knew about the lifeboats. Each day she glanced slyly to see if her little bird had begun to puff out.

Frustrated, Arkady spoke to the savvy sailor from whom he purchased pipe tobacco for Stefan. The sailor relished giving advice on life in America, where he'd not spent more than six weeks in a decade. Hearing about his country mainly from his mates, or the various people with whom he spent his leave, he felt free to filter the stray facts through his rather voluptuous imagination and create an idealized motherland. This mythic colony, a collage of Newark, Seattle, and Dallas, he contemplated each night before sleep, and in the end it completely displaced the unhappy memories of his Ohio home. The result was that Arkady returned from their conference grinning, as if he had just bought a choice plot in Valhalla, and said, simply, "New Jersey!"

Garden States

Clean Livings

THEIR SPONSOR, who told immigration officials he had jobs for Arkady and Stefan, worked as an usher in a re-run movie house on Bleeker Street in New York. While Arkady looked for work, Stefan and Natalka sat in the theater watching *King Kong*.

The giant gorilla pounded at the gates. The villagers shouted and shook their spears. They couldn't stop it. The doors burst open. The monster glared at the little people. Finally the Americans drugged it. But they made the mistake of bringing it to New York. Leave it, thought Stefan; you don't need it. Nobody listened. Suddenly there was Kong, climbing the Empire State Building. Fay Wray writhed in its fist. Natalka snored.

The first to find work, Lastivka took a job as a clean-ing woman in a midtown office building. She rode the A train. Her fellow passengers reminded her of the lu-natics in Vienna. One morning a man began reading from the Bible while boys in black leather jackets pounded the glass out of the windows with bats. When they reached Twenty-third Street, Lastivka got off, hurried over to the other side of the tracks and took the next train back. She swore to Arkady she'd never leave the apartment again.

Within days, however, she began going to St. George's Church on St. Mark's Place. There she volunteered to work with several women's groups raising money for the old country. They held raffles, bake sales, bazaars. The same people came to the events over and over. It was surprisingly easy to live in America without ever meeting Americans. The only time one ran into them was while shopping. Best of all, nobody cared what language one spoke. That was a big difference between here and there.

Arkady had trouble keeping a job. He moved furniture, drove newspapers to Long Island, pumped jelly into donuts. He kept getting fired because of his temper. He was trapped and he knew it. Speaking to a clerk in a hardware store, or to a fellow worker, or a boss, he listened closely for the least echo of condescension. One Sunday at mass he met Edward Zaremba, Lastivka's cousin, who worked at the SeaLand Plant in Newark. Edward took Arkady out and introduced him to the foreman. Before Arkady knew it, everything was settled. That's how it went in America. It was who you knew that counted. But the job was unionized; the benefits were good: who was he to complain?

I'd *like* to have a child, Arkady thought, standing before the mirror tying his tie.

In the kitchen Lastivka handed him a brown paper

bag with his liverwurst sandwich and a thermos of pea soup.

She had wanted a child ever since quitting her job.

"And don't get wet," she joked. She'd never seen the SeaLand Plant, but she imagined her husband working on a spit of land in the middle of the sea.

A child. The money. A child to keep the family name alive. The money. A child to fight their enemies. The money. A child to whom they'd pass on all they'd learned about this hard business of living. Not everything gets done in just one generation. Some dreams take several lifetimes of work. And the money.

That night in bed he put his hand on Lastivka's breast.

Later, she said, "If it's a girl, her name will be Theodosia. If it's a boy, we'll call him Bohdan." She turned her nose up for a kiss.

"It's happened, old girl," Stefan said to the comatose Natalka, who'd planted herself in the kitchen. She stirred only for food and sleep.

"Hmmmm?"

"You will soon be a grandmother. Maybe that will wake you up."

Natalka opened her eyes. She smiled. "What a shame."

"I know what you mean," Stefan said. "But they have to go through it themselves. And I, it seems, will have to find work after all." He'd spent every afternoon of the last week watching Robert Donat in the *Prisoner of Zenda*.

Every once in a while, walking down Second Avenue,

he'd see someone he'd known in Rozdorizha or the camps. Sometimes they'd stop to talk.

"Are you going to the meeting on Friday?"

"I have to work."

"They say Stalin is sick."

"May he die a thousand deaths."

Just as often, though, the people pretended they didn't recognize their acquaintances from the old world. In America they had the right to forget.

For weeks before going into labor, Lastivka prayed more earnestly than ever. She made God promise He'd care for her first born in a way He'd never tended anyone else. This was, after all, *her* child. Follow him like air, she said to God. I know You will, she added, more meekly, because of Your goodness.

At home, the boy in the crib, Stefan asleep on a couch in one corner of the room, Natalka in another, the tired parents huddled under the tent they'd set up over their mattress, which lay on the floor.

"He'll make music . . . "

"He'll make money . . . "

"God will help."

"God had better."

Alone with her son, Lastivka whispered, "Remember: you are the son of kings, and your children after you shall be kings."

Soon after Bohdan's birth, Arkady bought a black Chrysler. The family began taking Sunday rides beyond the city, exploring the other shore. They often went with Lastivka's cousins, the Zarembas. After months of looking, the couples found an affordable two-family home.

The Earthly Paradise

NEW JERSEY was heaven.

Starting across the river from New York, in Hackensack, and trailing down to Bayonne and Jersey City, then banding the center to Camden, bordering on Philadelphia, it was a factory without walls, webbed with conveyor belts passing for highways, down which raced the millions of parts needed to keep America running. A third of the country lived here. New Jersey took earth's raw materials and turned them into products. It was the cradle of consumerism. It gave the world paint, beer, petrochemicals, and endless lines of free-verse poets. All profited. Cows on Argentine ranches chewed laxatives from Rahway while their owners swilled Buds in Madrid, and the future president of Czechoslovakia drank in the chants of the scatological prophet from Newark.

The garbage heaped high. And flowered. The Garden State. Along highways, in towns. Even the new shopping centers sported gardens. Hyssop, dandelions, hollyhocks. Near factories, in cities Engels would have recognized, mullein and pokeweed bloomed from the sidewalk. And could enough ever be said about the suburbs? Veterans of foreign wars, having glimpsed human nature up close, crafted havens where their children grew safe as chimps in a zoo.

In 1950 the United States had six percent of the world's population and sixty percent of its wealth. Truman was president. There were anti-British riots in Egypt. Sixteen thousand people fled from East to West Berlin in a month. Schweitzer lived. So did Stalin. Locusts plagued Morocco, hurricanes the Caribbean. Only thirty million people in the world owned televisions and most of them lived around New Jersey. Europe and America felt crazy. Postwar syndrome. Grasshoppers and crickets were everywhere. Lightning bugs winked while silvery moths that shed a drizzle of powder wherever they landed rushed at the candles the emigrés set out on the redwood table in their yard in Free Fall.

And the technology.

"What did I tell you? Here everybody gets his own orchestra," Arkady cried when the Blaupunkt, their first stereo, was delivered. "Stereo," Lastivka whispered, listening to Chopin.

Above all, surrounding all, the ocean. The Atlantic, named for the continent it had swallowed, brimmed with waters from Bremen, Hamburg, and the Black Sea. No matter where in New Jersey you lived, water was near.

———

The house in Free Fall was double-chimneyed, white, and rested like a three-layered wedding cake in the center of a green serving tray. Built at the turn of the century, it boasted a screenless front porch behind pines which overtopped chimneys and hid it from its peers. The eastern yard supported a modest orchard of plum and apple and cherry and peach trees, none of which, thanks to the squirrels and jays, ever mothered a mature fruit. From among them rose an ancient, sickly mulberry whose hive-shaped fruits appalled the animal population. In the back, prefaced by a sparsely graveled drive, stood a carriage house converted to a garage. Hoofprints were stamped into the floorboards near a hitching post. There were saw horses, crusty slats of a once white picket fence, three red wheelbarrows, and the dust of a parrot named Sydney.

But the Vorogs lived on an island created by Arkady. His will, his dream, kept them from seeing the world around them.

Even Gwen McDonald, who lived in the maroon-shingled house on North Burdock, was repulsed. Gwen's family had been in Free Fall since the late 1700s. When the Vorogs arrived, noblesse oblige prompted her to visit them with local newspapers and carefully articulated advice on how they might enroll in the community. Arkady listened patiently while she explained about the PTA, the stamp club, gun club, canoe club, the senior citizens (for Stefan and Natalka), and other local organizations. After she left, the matter was dropped. There wasn't time for it. Why adjust to a country in which you were, at best, temporary residents?

With the exception of Gwen, the neighbors didn't know how to react to the Vorogs. People suspected these curious types, these Russians. That was what most of the locals decided they were — despite Arkady's passionate protestations that it was from the Russians they'd escaped.

Occasionally Dr. William Kaiser would be out in the next yard, trimming his junipers, while Stefan led a visitor down to see the rabbit. In approximate English, Stefan introduced Dr. Kaiser to General So-and-So, ambassador to Holland under the Austro-Hungarian Empire. Pleasure to meet a professional man. An ambassador? How splendid. Now selling bicycles in Elizabeth (three speeds the fashion)? No matter. Life. Wheel of fortune. Oh, these damned junipers. Nature would be wonderful if only she'd let things stay still a while.

Later Dr. Kaiser saw the former ambassador swinging upside down from the mulberry, making chimp noises to amuse some women, who cooed, "See the silly monkey! Give him a nut! Give him a nut!"

The neighbors were tolerant, as only Americans living in suburbia, surrounded by a carnival of customs and mystifying traditions, had learned to be. If finally they turned from these new settlers, who seemed unable to melt into agreeable molds, still the neighbors rarely called the police, and only when the cries coming from the house seemed to demand it.

———

Once, after discovering Orion, Dr. Kaiser invited himself to the Vorogs' for dinner.

Dr. Kaiser, as everyone but the Vorogs knew, was a lush twice investigated by the AMA because of complaints lodged by female patients.

He was their first American guest.

"What will I cook?" Lastivka wailed.

"What you always do."

"He'll want hamboorger hot dogs."

"Make them."

"I can't."

"Then what?"

They screamed at each other right up to the ring of the doorbell.

Arkady asked the good doctor to bring his wife, but was told that no, he couldn't do that, his wife never went anywhere. He did not say why. This seclusion seemed regular practice with American women, who avoided the outdoors as though the air swarmed with diseases. They could be seen only in supermarkets.

It was a warm evening. The doctor wore a blue seersucker suit, crimson tie, and glossy black wingtips. He smiled broadly (he was blotto) and seemed not to notice the sweat pouring down Arkady's face.

Lastivka prepared borscht, carp, *galupci,* and Linzertorte. Whenever there was a lull in the conversation, Arkady arched an eyebrow, signaling Lastivka to bring another course.

Blind to the anxiety fermenting around him, Kaiser slurped the soup and forked the fish and drank a fourth glass of *Liebfraumilch.*

He was celebrating. He would tell them about it presently. First he described in detail the layout of his summer home in the Poconos and the cottage he and his wife rented on Long Beach Island each July and recounted stories about their last trip to Switzerland. Had they ever been to Switzerland? No? But weren't they close? Yes, very. (Arkady was late for work. Lastivka worried the *holubci* were too thick with onions.) Late in life, the doctor said, he had turned to astronomy for entertainment and metaphysical solace. He knew of course that the only way one could claim to know something was if one learned it for oneself. So he decided to see if the stars in the sky really submitted to the laws he'd read about, or whether the whole thing wasn't the bluff of some advertising agency. He suspected that if the books were right, then there was order in the world: surely the earth behaved in congruence with the heavens. He'd made some original discoveries. He kept patting his bald head. "You can't tell with the naked eye, but if you study it using a good telescope" (he had a Bausch and Lomb), "You'll see the handle on the little dipper is chipped." He saw part of it fly off one night. Lastivka and Arkady shook their heads, incredulous. Stefan scowled, biting his tongue.

"Why not publish your account?" Arkady asked.

"If the government doesn't want the public to know, there must be a reason," he explained.

Arkady and Lastivka nodded. "Of course there must be a reason."

After an hour, Arkady's shirt was soaked with sweat. He had to repeat every sentence three times.

"It's near Poland."

"Beg pardon?"

"R-O-Z-D-O-R-I-Z-H-A."

"Beg pardon?"

"First we were in Berchtesgaden, then . . . "

"How do you spell that?"

"B-E-R-C-H-T-E-S-G-A-D-E-N."

"Sounds German."

"It is."

"That's where we met, the wife and I."

"Oh, you're not from the same country?"

"Yes, but we met in the camp."

"One of those DP camps?"

"Yes."

"And were you in that camp, too, Mr. Zabobon?"

"Ah, yes."

"And where were you before that?"

"P-A-R-I-S . . . "

"France?"

When the door shut, Arkady went over and kicked the dog. That was the last American ever to enter the house.

Money

For Arkady, ownership ushered in the black decades of mortgage and overtime, busted furnaces and leaky roofs, bitter mornings and sad evenings, silent hearts and run-down bodies.

"Money-money-money," he swore.

"Beware of the blindness," Stefan, bon vivant, Plato-bloated lecher, counseled.

Lastivka and Arkady were always fighting. "I demand an allowance," she cried, kicking her chair.

"What do you need? I'll buy it for you."

"No, I want to buy it myself."

She had taken up sewing again. A spare room on the third floor was stocked with boxes of crepes and brightly patterned synthetics and lime-green cottons.

"You heard me," Arkady growled.

"Peasant! We should never have married. Castes don't mix well."

After a fight she shut herself in the bathroom. Arkady, raging, grabbed a butter knife and tried unscrewing the lock.

Bo sat at the dinner table in his high chair, unable to leave.

Stefan was right, though: Arkady's blood was perfect. Despite frequent flare-ups, it rarely occurred to him he wasn't responsible for feeding whoever happened to be living in the house.

Since he didn't drink, his only release came from shouting. He was constantly in a rage. Arguing over a phone bill, he leapt up and hit Lastivka, sending her back two steps before she found her balance and stopped. She stared, saying nothing, gray eyes ice, and then she spat, her phlegm missing his face, landing on his coat collar.

He turned, walked out. The grass needed cutting, and he walked to the garage and dragged out the mower, pulled the cord, once, twice, finally the engine started, spitting smoke, and he drove it in. Bitch.

He suffered because of the wall around him. His rage was the wall, and his rage was the ram with which to knock it down. Bitch. All you know is yourself and what you want. What do you know? Here the bosses treat you like the Russians did. The bondage is subtle. They say you can move between classes. But you can't do it without killing who you are. He plunged the mower into the grass, sucking in the smell of it. I hate you, you selfish bitch, he mouthed, the wind drying the sweat beading his face. Slavery everywhere. He was a slave to Kopf at work. He was a slave to his wife because he said "I love you" to her, and the words were cuffs, keeping him there, locking the two of them together at the heart. Worst of all, he never talked about this to anyone. He hardly talked to anyone. He wanted to leave his wife.

But a man was only as good as his word. If he broke it, who would he be? He stooped to study a caterpillar inching across a stone, its furry body rising, swelling up into a question mark. What did it need to know? How to live? Get along with a woman who seemed determined to kill him with her complaints? As though he didn't work all the time, as though he hadn't taken on more than he could handle by moving to the suburbs in the first place. They belonged back in the ghetto on the Lower East Side. How much did everyone expect of him? To work without love? It was affection that nourished a man. Not sleep and food. But this wasn't the woman he fell in love with. What obligation did strangers have to each other? He wanted to say, "I don't know you. Leave me alone. Who are you to ask these things?" It made him sick: her skin had coarsened; her hair was dyed. She no longer liked making love. But when she said she wanted her own bed, he shook his huge head no, saying that when he stopped being able to reach out at night to touch her, they would no longer be married.

If he wanted to sleep with someone else, why not? But he was afraid of adultery, so he went to a pornographic film in New York. It calmed and sickened him. He felt sated and poisoned by the plunge into pure fantasy, in watching actions performed as though they had no consequences. Still lust gripped him. At work he pushed his broom but his mind stalked the plump soft girl he saw on the street hours before. One day he was driving back from the Ukrainian National Home in New York. He'd gone there to watch a soccer match on television. While he waited at a traffic light near the Holland Tunnel, someone rapped on the window. A tall blonde woman, thick-lipped, eyes shaded green, smiled at him. *La Traviata* poured from the radio. *Sacrificio,* Alfredo's father boomed in a fit of paternal meddling. The blonde wore a yellow top that clung to her breasts like rubber and a black skirt that sheathed her legs to the tops of her thighs. She smiled. She crooked a finger at him, pointed it at herself, then pressed the scarlet fingernail down on a risen nipple. *Addio de passato,* Violetta sang. She began rolling up her top. Arkady was all muscle and bone staring at the bottom sweep of her breasts, then at the nipples themselves. As a final test of his loyalty, the woman began to hike up her skirt. The baying of horns cut short his pleasure. The cars behind were bored. They'd seen the show before.

The memory made him tremble. He considered going to confession to tell the priest, but he believed in God, not in priests.

He drove the mower through the long hair of the grass. The engine roared so loud he barely heard himself think. He saw an image of his mother at the train station, her skirt pulled over her head by the soldiers, and he drove the mower forward, deeper, thrusting and thrusting into America.

Then the mower died. He yanked at the cord. Nothing.

———

For years Lastivka tried to avoid looking in store windows. Sometimes she couldn't help it, though. So when she saw a skirt or a blouse she wanted, she said a Hail

Mary. She had her own sewing room, but that wasn't the same as buying clothes stitched in Taiwan or Paris. The women in the magazines always had new clothes to go with the smiles. Their lives seemed so bright, affectionate, and orderly. She read their stories and imitated their recipes, but it did not make a difference.

If only she were more beautiful. She'd been pretty enough for the old world. But here men preferred perfect pictures to blemished flesh. In America, they made goddesses.

She spent what little money she had on wigs. The first she bought in a department store in Elizabeth. It was red and synthetic. Her second was animal hair. After Stefan took a job as a clerk at Woolworth's, he was able to get them for her at a discount.

She loved them partly because she knew she'd never wear them. Arkady wouldn't let her.

Her collection grew. Soon she had wigs in every color. She bought a few styrofoam heads. After Arkady left for work, she placed them around the bedroom. She confided to them that her husband was a brute and she was lonely. Sometimes her father flickered at the edges of her sight, leaning on the doorjamb, smiling.

Her husband was the real test of her virtue. She'd sealed herself off from anything that might give him pleasure. She hated coffee because he loved it, wouldn't sing to him because he had no ear. Why hadn't they known this about each other sooner? They both felt the same isolation. She talked to her plants, her wigs, and her father's ghost. People didn't understand. She told the wigs she believed she'd marry only after becoming a famous actress. Was it the war? The strange way it lit

things, giving them a meaning they did not by themselves have?

She loved the tabloids. Stories about dogs giving
birth to children, politicians who were half man and half
lizard, Martian visitations. She paid particular attention to stories about wives who'd killed their husbands.
The violence in her mind frightened her.

She guiltily recalled the story a nun told her about St.
Theresa of Avila, who fell off the donkey while riding to
Rome. The saint heard God say, "That is how I treat my
friends." To which the self-possessed woman answered,
"And that is why Thou hast so few of them." Wasn't she
herself like St. Theresa? Hadn't God given her an impossible life? Her father had been shot, and her country
had been stolen, but she loved the Lord and went to
mass daily and urged her husband to go.

Instead, Arkady fought with her about everything.
They couldn't have a peaceful morning.

"Can we go to the country Sunday?"

"What? When? Impossible."

The answer was like a slap. It made her want to hurt
him. Why? Was this the way Zenon and Natalka had
acted with each other?

"When will you take me to the ocean?" she'd ask, trying to wring a concession from him.

Good thing he worked; if he stayed home, they'd have
surely killed each other.

She herself no longer worked with church groups as
much as she had when they were in the city.

She asked Natalka once, "Is marriage supposed to be
like this?"

Her mother fluttered open her lids. "What, dear?"

"Were you and Father like this?"

"Worse, darling. He was always getting shot. And before that he lectured me. Long, stupid lectures. He told me what to think about music, the grass, my dreams. He didn't even leave me my dreams. I destroyed his whole library. Darling, it's war. Don't worry, it's natural."

Spent, Natalka closed her eyes and tumbled back into a light sleep. In her dreams King Toor, who looked like King Kong, made love to her from behind.

Lastivka turned to her father's ghost, whom she could barely see through the cloud of smoke.

"Don't worry," he said. "It's just that right from the start, from the moment they're born, men are different. They're told to be different. And they end up that way. Men and women use the same language, but their words don't stand for the same things. They never bother to find out what the other one means. There's never time. Life is like a film in which the projector is constantly racing. But in life there's no freeze frame. No way to reverse what happens. If you walk out in the middle, you don't see how it ends.

"That's a fine invention, the movies. You live near the inventor's home, you know."

"I know. I have been to Hollywood."

"No, dear. Thomas Alva Edison. Edison, New Jersey."

Staking a tomato, she thought: at least they were all traveling through this strangeness together. Arkady, Bo, Stefan, Natalka.

She looked at the radishes, the eggplant, the pole beans. She ripped at the weeds. Maybe marriage was a mistake. Men and women weren't meant to live together. Their rhythms were too different. If only she felt just one way, either hated him or loved him.

They'd gone through so many stages. Sometimes they were close as folded socks. Then they were as cold and limp to each other as old coats hung side by side in a closet. She couldn't bear being near him. The clerk in the supermarket knew her better.

Why should she tell Arkady anything? He had no tenderness. All he wanted was sex. As long as they made love, all was well. But in those periods when she felt the vital independence of her body, felt she needed to keep her mouth and breasts and sex to herself, he grew furious.

She hated her husband for keeping her trapped, and she had her mother's capacity for resentment.

Just when she thought she was ready to leave him, she'd recall their earliest days. He'd been so sweet when he offered her his light bulb. And how strong he seemed in the camp. He'd been the commandant's favorite. He knew how to deal with the men on the black market. He took care of her mother. Natalka had told her God sent angels to protect you. Was he one of the angels? On the boat on a cold night he bought her a cashmere coat, and then he got that Italian from Romania to snap their picture with his Brownie. Six months later the photos arrived at Pavlichko's apartment. And those days in New York — not so long ago — when she cried before going to work. She'd been more scared than during the war. The softer her life became, the more anxious she grew. Maybe it was a delayed reaction. She'd read about something called free-floating anxiety. Would life ever become what she thought it should be?

She wiped her hands on the old apron and stood up.

A hawk circled overhead. Over this tame land.

But it was not tame; there was a wildness underneath things.

"I want to die," she'd say to her mother.

"That's a sin."

"Lord forgive me, it's true!"

Yet how soft Arkady was around Bo right after the birth. He reminded Natalka of Zenon after he'd been shot.

Late one morning, she stood outside smelling the lemony laundry while Bo played in the sandbox.

The day before, there'd been a story in the local papers about a child who was playing quietly in his yard in Free Fall when a stranger walked by and stuck a knife in the boy's heart. She read it to Natalka after Arkady left for work. In a few years Bo would start school, and then how would she protect him? Only the island of home was safe. Even there the world crept in, concealed in the evening papers. When her cousin Edward Zaremba, who lived on the first floor, brought home a huge used Zenith, she saw up close places she'd never known existed: Korea, Tibet, Rhodesia. Everywhere fires blazed—Castro in Cuba, Russians everywhere. Those same fires she believed had gone out at the end of the war flared in other places around the world. The refuge was vulnerable.

She believed God sent the war to teach the Europeans a lesson, but nobody ever learned.

Bo was only five but sometimes he thought about God. God was in church on Sundays. He liked watching the man in gold and white robes saying words he couldn't understand. He especially liked the church at night when it was cold and smelled of leaves and smoke, far nicer than that terrible stuff from Uncle Stefan's pipe. The stained glass windows were dark and the priest talked to the people as to friends. The candles shimmered with haloes. Bo asked his mother about God, and she told him that God was watching him all the time and that he should pray every night and morning.

"Who are you talking to?" Lastivka asked Bo, who crouched in his sandbox.

"The soldiers are quarreling. Like you and Father."

Suddenly Lastivka felt someone's eyes on them. Was it her father? She looked around. Nothing but the dogwood buffeting in the wind.

Then she turned to her neighbor's house and saw Mrs. Kaiser in her kitchen window. What did the woman want? Bees moved among the dandelions, and why was the woman staring? She grew scared. "Come, son." They fled into the house.

Bo put on the grasshopper costume he'd worn to the Ukrainian Children's Ball. Lastivka slipped Chopin onto the Blaupunkt. She told Bo to put his feet on top of hers. They danced.

Arkady was not a superstitious man. Unlike Lastivka, he never prayed to St. Christopher when he lost something. (She held other suspect ideas too. For example, she believed she had some influence on the weather. When the sky darkened, she pouted silently in the kitchen, braiding paskas or stuffing *holubci*. If the clouds passed, she said quietly, "It stormed all right. But it happened here, in me. I took the thunder in. The lightning and the thunder and the wind." And she confessed to Bo that when she met his father, she felt closer to the trees. "I placed my hand on a poplar and it moved under my fingers. Then I pressed my cheek against it. I could hear its heart." It might have been all the ghosts she picked up from sitting around cemeteries. They had rubbed themselves into her feet, her calves; they clung to her skirt and clamored for her attention.) And Arkady never quarreled with sprites and ariels while wading through leaves under the arched chestnuts of Berry Street, as did his neighbor, Edward Zaremba's wife, Lilka, a self-proclaimed white witch who worked as a nurse's aide and who was known to the citizens of Free Fall, for some obscure reason, as Sam. But if Lilka's mind was stocked with numerous strange notions that were like groupers in a world accustomed to goldfish, Arkady too had one odd bird flitting about his brain.

One day he decided a ritual was necessary to keep the past alive. Daily, after dinner, he insisted that Lastivka sit at the yellow-blue piano (he had painted it, the colors of the Ukrainian flag). Stefan and Natalka sank back onto the plastic-enveloped cushions of the sofa. Clearing his throat, Bo climbed his perch on the blue end table. Following a few introductory chords, Lastivka sang, in a voice passionate as that of the guitarist in *Casablanca*, belting out the *Marseillaise*: *Sche ne vmerla Ukraina* . . .

The national anthem. Arkady, unlike Victor Lazlo, would not join in. He stood near the Blaupunkt, head back, face motionless but for the toothpick shuttling like an inquisitive periscope from one corner of his mouth to the other.

At the end he commented, "You were off-key, nightingale," or "*Fortissimo*, Slava, *fortissimo!*" And they began again. Once, during their fourth encore, he glanced at his watch and, seeing he would be late for work, quietly left the room. They heard only the thunder of the door behind him. Stefan had fallen silent after the second chorus. Suddenly he rose from the couch and, leaning heavily on his dolphin-handled cane, said to Lastivka, "He's not a bad man, Slava, but this . . . ," he paused to let his finger tap a telegram on his temple, "this is plain kookoo-na-moonyu."

Friday mornings, after the family returned from shopping together, they surrounded the dining room table with bags. Lastivka pulled their purchases out one by one and announced the prices: forty-nine cents/D (for dairy, and so on). Arkady solemnly scanned the scrolled receipts and X-ed the appropriate faint blue hieroglyphs with his red pen. This process took them to mid-afternoon. If, at the end, a line of figures remained unmarked, he hurried into his black Chrysler and drove back to the A&P. Sometimes he brought Bo along as a character reference. Haggling with the droopy-eyed clerk wearing a Snuffy Smith T-shirt, Arkady made the boy, blushing and ashamed, stand in front of him, as if to say, "You think a tree capable of producing such an apple could be rotten enough to lie?"

Up until Bo turned twelve, his father nourished in both their minds the crazy idea that one day they would invade the Ukraine and liberate her from her oppressors. All of them would retire to a village south of Rozdorizha and raise geese. This was what Stefan called his "kookoo-na-moonyu."

How would they do it? With guns, cunning, a vigilante legion inducted from dreams? On this point he stayed mute. "When the time comes," he whispered darkly.

Meanwhile they had to keep in shape. At dawn Arkady appeared by the boy's bed, a darker sun, worrying Bo's shoulder with his massive hand. Half-asleep, Bo would sigh to the floor and do sit-ups, whimpering, "Daddy, why?" Then, jumping jacks. Followed by pushups. At that hour Arkady might have shown some mercy toward his only child, but he didn't really notice who Bo was until much later.

Arkady had doubts about the enterprise. What, finally, did national identity matter? Weren't countries illusory categories? Sometimes he wished he'd been born a Jew, an Irishman, an Italian. They had earned the privilege of being seen. Before the world could see you, however, it needed the right words with which to name you. He feared America was tired of the clamor of small republics and exhausted nations, each shouting more loudly than the next, *I am*. Besides, what was there to say about a country which had seen its best days 700 years ago?

But there were feelings that "natives," people who'd rooted themselves, took for granted. Every immigrant stepped off the Mayflower. It took a generation of wrestling with the angel-demon of the soil before a plot of earth let you claim it. So many contradictions. Should a man stay free — landless, countryless — worshipping exclusively the holy spirit, no matter where it arose? Truth was, this couldn't be done. The soul saw through the body's eyes and felt affection only for particular trees, people, skylines. Some saintly types might successfully detach themselves, claiming kinship with the universal sun and the common sky, the same everywhere: but even Christ stayed in Galilee. He did not rush to Rome seeking a larger audience. Being Ukrainian was another way of being alone.

While other kids played softball and went to the movies and did their homework, Bo studied how to be a Ukrainian.

Friday nights he went to Ukrainian Boy Scouts, where he learned to tie knots, stand at attention, sing songs, and find his way out of treacherous forests. Saturdays he studied the grammar, history, literature, and geology of Ukraine, with a special emphasis on Rozdorizha.

At school, while other kids talked about the Yankees or *I Spy,* he listened closely and wondered if his father would ever buy a television. He began smuggling in copies of *Spiderman* comics, which he hid at the bottom of his toy box.

———

Father "Smoking Joe" Brodin, a coal miner's son from Willowsburg, Pennsylvania, was heading for the major leagues until a shattered knee brought him nearer to God, who, in time, sent him to Elizabeth, New Jersey. Rough and driven, he quickly connected with his parishoners, whose hardscrabble lives reminded him of his parents and the mines.

He loved cigars. In one shirt pocket, he carried a rosary, in the other a Panatella. Once the altar boys played a joke on him: during an Easter blessing he reached for his miter so he could sprinkle his people with holy water, and instead he wound up waving a cigar at the crowd. He was eager to please his superiors and his flock felt sure they'd soon lose him to a greener pasture. In the meantime, they listened earnestly to his sermons.

On Saturday night he sat at his desk leafing through the crumbling brown cloth Bible his mother had given him when he graduated from sixth grade.

He was puzzled by the text around which he'd chosen to build his sermon. It was Genesis 4, which he thought he knew bottom to top. Cain and Abel. Cain slew Abel and was punished—what else was there to it?

But he couldn't keep straight in his mind which one was Cain and which Abel. The names didn't stick. And why did God reject Cain's offering? Father remembered tortured sociological talk at the seminary about how the passage described man's transition from hunter-gatherer to farmer. But that didn't make sense. Cain was the farmer. Why did God put him in such a situation?

And what did this passage mean? "If thou doest well, shalt thou not be accepted? And if thou doest not well, sin lieth at the door. And unto thee shall be his desire, and thou shalt rule over him."

What was God suggesting? That power had the right to take what it wanted?

He lit a cigar.

When Mrs. Sigalsky asked if he wanted tea before she left, he almost invited her in to discuss the business. But he was not in the habit of revealing his weaknesses. He sat up late, alone, glancing at the Book on his desk, thinking about Mrs. Pavlichko's asthma, and the choir, and the *pirohy* sale. Then he wandered over to the RCA, switched it on, and sat down.

"Brothers and sisters in Christ, you may remember James Dean in *East of Eden* saying to Jason Robards: 'I'm not my brother's keeper.' You probably recognize the words from today's introit.

"Burl Ives goes on to quote Genesis: 'And Cain went out from the presence of the Lord, and dwelt in the land of Nod, on the east of Eden.' Then he tells Dean to get out of town.

"It sounds simple enough. But if we look at the passage closely, brothers and sisters, if we stop to think about it, we'll see that its meaning is far from obvious, far from simple."

He glanced into the crowded pews of odd hats and cheap dresses and worn gray suits. His people. The second war had created hundreds of thousands of emigrés. It had brought new life to the church. Out of suffering sprang faith.

"In fact, when you sit down and read the chapter, you may find yourselves a little puzzled, as I myself was last night.

"Cain complains to God that his punishment is too much. 'Behold,' he says, 'thou hast driven me out this day from the face of the earth; and from thy face shall I be hid; and I shall be a fugitive and a vagabond in the earth; and it shall come to pass, that every one that findeth me shall slay me.' And God in his infinite mercy puts a mark on him to tell others not to do as he has done. He tells Cain, 'Therefore whosoever slayeth Cain, vengeance shall be taken on him sevenfold.' God makes Cain into a negative example.

"This is a terrible punishment. Imagine the world seeing you as the man who murdered his own brother. Imagine living your whole life as an example of what men must not be. Every stranger you meet thinks to himself: I never want to be like this.

"None of us is an island unto himself, brothers and sisters. Whenever we think we are, our souls shrivel.

"Now the Bible is a tough book. It's a book that has to be read over and over. Remember, Cain doesn't just disappear. He gets married, has kids. They all live for hundreds of years. Methuselah, who makes it to 869, outliving Adam by 39 years, is a descendant of Cain's.

"So what does it add up to? That it pays to kill your brother? That God rewards you for it with a nice wife and plenty of grandchildren? Sometimes it looks that way.

"Many of you have been cast out of your gardens by the Communists. Does that make you like Cain? No. We all know in our hearts that you are not like Cain.

"You think you've lost it all. You see yourselves as losers in this deal. You've lost your families, your homes, your land, your country. But listen to me. It's the Communists who are the losers. They are the ones God has cast out of His garden. They are the ones who bear the mark of Cain.

" 'So what?' you might ask. Didn't they steal your lands and kill your fathers and mothers?

"Even so, my good people, the Communists are the ones who bear the mark of Cain. And that means a lot. Because it is far better to be killed than to be a killer.

"One last point. It was Abel's offering God accepted. And it was Abel Cain slew. And it was to God Abel went. Here, my people, is the strange conclusion to which this leads me. We know in our hearts that the rewards of the world are empty. The worst thing that we can do is to lead a life out of harmony with the word of God. What if Death itself, when it is righteous, when it is for a just cause, is a blessing?

"In the name of the Father, the Son, and the Holy Ghost. Amen."

───────────

After mass Arkady decided to show Lastivka where he worked. For years he'd wanted to take somebody from the family to the plant. But no one ever volunteered. No one seemed interested. As long as he came home Thursday with the paycheck, who cared where it came from? Now he wanted his wife to see the place in which he spent so many hours.

When they passed the Hollywood delicatessen, Lastivka said, "I didn't know we were so near Hollywood."

Arkady laughed. "There," he pointed to the massive

gray building emblazoned with the company trade-mark, a red neon seal intertwined with a glowing blue ampersand.

"How . . . impressive. It's so big," Stefan said, nudging Lastikva.

Arkady glanced at his wife.

"Hideous."

The toothpick dissolved. He sped on.

"I wouldn't say that," said Stefan.

"No, dear, no," Natalka added. "And look at that nice parking lot. And what's that across the street? Tents?"

"The hoboes."

"What are they?"

"Men who've had enough."

A few days before, having arrived at work early, Arkady had crossed the street and walked into the shanty town.

Local factories used the lot as a dump. He passed oil drums, mangled shopping carts, heaps of clothes. One hill was built of gloves, another of tires, another of shoes. He passed what looked like a house with a hood for a roof. A cat curled on a three-legged chair. The air was charged with the amber light of desperation. The cords in his neck tightened. Why would anyone leave home for this?

Men huddling round a fire made no sign of having seen him.

He looked at their faces. Poverty and weather perfected them. In the firelight their skin looked brownish. They reminded him of the faces of the men he'd met at a work camp in Germany after the war. Need and desire solidified in the bone.

A man wearing a Yankees cap glanced at him. Arkady started to smile, but the man looked away.

Another man, who'd been drinking from a thermos, stood up and glared at Arkady.

Fifty feet away trucks roared down Route 1.

"How 'had enough'?" Lastivka asked.

"Headaches, problems. They've had enough."

"What do they think? Life should be fun? You shouldn't talk like that in front of Bo."

"Let him see."

To Bo the factory looked like a castle. There had to be dragons nearby.

"Look, a Coca-Cola truck," Bo cried. The boy began shouting: "Look, look, look . . . "

"Shut up," Arkady shouted.

He turned off the highway and took the long way home through the park. On happier Sundays the family had picnicked on the lake under the willow.

Arkady's job became something of a family secret. Lastivka wouldn't talk about it. It was ugly, and ugliness had no place in her home.

At four o'clock Arkady returned to the plant where he traded his Sunday suit for blue overalls.

All evening (and sometimes all night), he walked among the stacked crates, through the monstrous warehouse lit by long tubes humming like angry cicadas. After everyone else had left, he sang. Ukrainian folk songs about dark girls, magic mountains, talking cranes. His words echoed through the warehouse, bounding off crates recently arrived from Italy, Portugal, Japan. The sound slipped into boxes of leather gloves from Florence and nested in crates of ceramics from Spain.

He loved sweeping. His favorite broom had a wide head. He picked it up with his right hand, carried it parallel to the ground, set it down gingerly, took the handle with both hands, letting the end stick out under his arm and pushed. The bristles against the tiles soothed him. He wiped his brow with his handkerchief. It was one of the purest professions. Like breathing. How many floors had he walked across in his life? No counting. In his father's barn he lay on the floor and made love to Melodia. He'd forgotten her. Her soft breasts. And the floor of the rowboat where he lay with Lastivka. Long ago, when they still made love. What happened to Rakovsky, the piano teacher? People changed. That was strange. He had not changed, though. He still recognized himself. He was the same man he had been on the farm and in the camps. Maybe he was rough with Bo, but you had to teach a boy the ways of the world. He wished he had more time for him, but there wasn't really time for anything except work. That was the first thing he had to teach his son. A poor man is always working. He tried a few bars of *Turandot*. Near midnight. How much time people spent alone. Astonishing. Nobody knew him.

The building itself changed. The walls sighed, the dark windows eyed him narrowly. Who was he? What language did he speak? Where was his passport? Did he know English? The pledge of allegiance? Last month they'd gone to the City Hall in Elizabeth to take their oath of citizenship. They came back carrying little flags in black plastic pedestals. Arkady poured everyone a glass of homemade Tokay. But their mood was cheerless, dark. He turned the Blaupunkt on to the shortwave. They sat around the rest of the evening listening to the broadcasts of Radio Free Europe. They'd begun to suspect that they would never go home.

———

Word spread: the Vorogs had an empty room in their attic.

Lastivka's cousins, Blind Peter and Teta Vera, inaugurated the migration, driving up to the house in a used but lustrous red Buick in which they'd lived for three months.

If there wasn't room for them indoors, Vera said, they'd sleep in the car. What they really needed was a safe place to park. New York was too dangerous. She pointed to where hubcaps once graced the tires.

"They were silver."

"Chrome," grunted Blind Peter.

"When did you get a license, Vera?"

"License?"

They insisted they could only stay a week. They remained through most of the winter until one morning in late February Vera declared bitterly that they were leaving for Florida, where it never snowed. As though the snow were Arkady's fault. Afterwards they returned yearly for Easter and Christmas.

Raised in the same provincial city in the southeastern part of Ukraine, Blind Peter and Vera had worked together as printers. Blind Peter, once eagle-eyed, rejoiced in the Revolution. He went to Moscow as a people's representative. Because he worked with his hands, he considered himself a poet of matter. The controllers of capital, who did nothing to enrich the earth, were middlemen, ivy on the windows, blocking the light. He didn't see the Revolution as a cruel thing. Their fall seemed as natural as the shearing of the ivy the moment the house again came into the hands of the living. The rich were robbed because they were oblivious to the suffering around them. They were all appetite. He was sorry, though, when nationalistic chauvinism poisoned class solidarity. Later, when several million peasants starved, he was furious with Stalin.

Vera's devotion to Peter was absolute. She shared his bed, his work, his opinions. She even wanted a part in his blindness.

One night Bo, dressed in a grasshopper costume, walked into the dark living room. When he switched on the lights, he saw Blind Peter and Teta Vera on the couch, holding hands.

"Why didn't you turn on the lights?" he asked Vera.

"I'm trying to see what it's like to be him," she explained.

Other visitors followed.

The spare room in the attic had no sooner been aired and the sheets changed and the circular stamp, left by the glass in which the last guest had soaked her teeth, polished out and the various bits of food—corn, apples, and prunes wrapped in handkerchiefs—cast into a pail for the compost heap, than the doorbell rang.

The visitors plotted and ate Arkady's food and drank his whiskey. Arkady and Lastivka refilled glasses and spent their days driving between home and the A&P.

When the weather was nice, they hung out near the mulberry in the back yard. Adriana Benko sang, accompanied by Pavlo Horak on the accordion. Silent Natalka sat in a lawn chair remembering the accordionist who let her touch the keys of his instrument so many centuries ago.

The trees listened to emigré gossip.

"They released Hawrylyuk, did you hear? Yes, the dissident historian, yes. He's in France. Near Paris. I hear he's half cracked. Maybe that's why they let him out. It seems he's training an army. Gagarin and Shepard canvas the stars, and our man gives boys Swiss army knives and cap guns and marches them around the Bois de Boulogne. They say he spends three hours each morning standing on his head. It's taking its toll."

Bo climbed up the mulberry. He was looking for the easel on which the sky rested. Someone had told him about it. He kept going higher. He felt the sun warming him, embracing him like a friend.

Hunched over the flowers, Arkady couldn't pull out his trowel. He leaned on the handle and the roots snapped. The trowel came out. He beat the wreath against the wooden basket, shaking off the soil.

He stood up, stretched his arms, still thick and muscled, scratched his chin, sighed. Things were worse at work. Kopf, fucking Kopf.

He looked at the garage that was about to collapse. He couldn't afford to repair it. Money. He glanced at his guests. Did they know how cheap the whiskey was? To pay for this he worked seven days a week. And everything was second rate. Not quite real. Money paid for reality. The real lasts.

Nobody knew the depth of his obsession. People claimed he'd given in to American materialism. But Arkady knew things were the same everywhere. In India, South Africa, Australia, the Soviet Union. Everyone worried about it. The concern was actual as roots. It was what bound one to the earth. Money had its own laws. They were unchangeable, definite as Nature's. Moreover, they were obeyed in a way that God's commandments never were.

But what did he know of the rich, who lived in a moral atmosphere so different from his they may as well have been from another planet? To others he denounced the Rockefellers and the Rothschilds as parasites, vampires: wasn't the Dracula myth a metaphor for the merciless way landlords sucked the blood of the peasants, and weren't bankers our twentieth-century version of the undead? Yet he respected them. He wished he could travel, swim in Hawaii, sink into the soft leather of a ruby-red limousine, know many girls, and all the continents. He counted out the things he'd never have: an electric reclining chair, a good stereo, free time. Merely naming the items pleased him. He ran through the inventory. His prophetic soul revealed pleasures his body would never know—and yet the soul itself, which had, Arkady knew, a separate existence, was self-sufficient, self-delighting. Lastivka had more religious insight than he did: in her eyes, everyone really was equal. But she never worked. She was free to breathe in the clean air of poetry and dreams. She had never grown up. He knew that even in church, prayers were supported with offerings. As for poetry, it was the leaf, the flower, completely dependent on the trunk.

He looked up at Bo and cried, "Careful!" Shaking his head he turned back to the azalea, its roots bundled in burlap.

One afternoon a crew of friends and relatives sat around the Vorogs' living room. The group included the twins, George and Pavlo.

"There's only one thing to do," said Uncle George, fingering the Indian headband he'd bought at the five and dime. ("Why do you people still dress like Europeans?" he said to Arkady. "It's time to assimilate.")

"What's that?" asked Pavlo, his twin.

"We must get Arkady to run for mayor."

"What are you talking about?" Pavlo pursued.

"In Czechoslovakia I ate a cat," George offered.

"In the Tyrol they're called roof rabbits."

"There were worms in my soup."

"People eat in restaurants all the time here."

"There's no other way. We will otherwise never accomplish our purpose," George said.

"Political power. I understand. But could we win?"

Pavlo worked in a luncheonette in Newark. George was unemployed. He blamed it on the Negroes.

"To control the ballot box!"

"Precisely. Precisely. We are an ancient culture. We must show them how to live."

"I was reading Madame Vovkoolaka the other day. She said you must meditate two hours each dawn . . . "

"Girls love me. They're always coming up . . . "

Bo turned from one to the other. They spoke urgently.

Arkady walked in. "Oh, a convention of Zabobons . . . Trying to raise fifty cents between you? Put me down for nothing." To Lastivka he said, "These shirts were on the stairs."

"I must have dropped them."

"Were you running away from Mrs. Kaiser again?"

"We think she's a spy," George said.

"Arkady, we think you should run for mayor."

Arkady stared at the middle-aged man in the Indian head band. "Don't push me, idiot."

"*Mensche brutalne!*"

"Woman!"

"You are."

"I'm telling you."

"You're telling me?"

"You can't even do laundry!"

"Oh, father . . . ," Lastivka cried, looking over her husband's shoulder toward Zenon, who stood there smiling, hands folded behind his back.

"Father? He's been dead twenty years. Don't you remember? He died so he could have another night with his whore. That seems to be a pattern in your family. Nobody works. Mistresses. The upper classes. The intelligentsia!"

Natalka snored in the chair, dreaming of Toor.

Bo started to cry.

"Look, you've scared him!"

"Stop crying, idiot!"

It began to rain.

"Good thing you took the laundry in," George said.

Rain and thunder.

"Let's listen to the radio," someone in the crowd suggested.

Arkady switched on the Blaupunkt.

"The president warns . . . to invade . . . and reprisals . . . "

"What about the bedroom windows?" Arkady said and left the room.

Stefan looked at Bo. "What are they teaching you in school?"

"On Top of Old Smoky," the boy answered, sniffling.

"What is that?" George grew excited at the prospect of more Americana.

"Yes, sing it."

"Do they teach you algebra yet?"

"I'm only in first grade."

"Americans! Wasting their time with smokings before teaching mathematics. There will be time for smokings later!"

"Both windows were open!" Arkady shouted, coming back in.

"What about geography? What's the capital of China?" Bo didn't know. "Peking, boy, Peking. Everybody should know that. The Chinese will rule the world one day. Then nobody will remember Washington."

"Let's really sing!" Lastivka suggested.

"Smoking, I want this smoking!"

They stared eagerly at Bo. "All right," he said glumly.

Within minutes the whole family, except for Arkady, who was getting ready for work, sat around the living room singing "On Top of Old Smoky."

"One of the niggers can sweep," Kopf, the foreman, said to Arkady. "I want you in the guardhouse. Stan's sick. He'll be out a few days."

Why was he offering him this? The guardhouse was a mint job. Kopf hated him.

Sure, he'd sub. But what was the real story here?

The next day he was in the booth watching the sun taxi down the airport runway across the street. The *Journal* lay on the table.

"Looks like Stan won't be back for a while. Maybe never."

Arkady had heard it was cancer.

Kopf looked toward the new terminals. It was going to be one of the busiest airports in the world. "Between you and me," he said (When had they grown so intimate? Arkady wondered), "I think it's cancer."

A new parking lot covered the dump where the hoboes once roosted.

"You like it here?"

"It's okay." He liked the break from sweeping. He liked reading, listening to opera on the tape deck.

"Something you can do for me though," Kopf said, dropping his voice, which was already low and conspiratorial.

Arkady tried reading the inscription inside the bottle tattooed on Kopf's forearm.

"A truck comes at three; you open the gate. That's it."

Arkady shrugged. Kopf shivered.

"Cold out here. I'm going in."

At five after three, an unmarked twelve-ton truck pulled up to the guardhouse and Arkady, sweating in the November damp, shut the gate behind it.

The moon watched over the airport.

He was working double shifts and by the time he got home, Bo had already left for school.

Lastivka woke him at three the next afternoon. She gave him coffee in a thermos and a sausage sandwich.

That night Kopf stopped by again. His thin lips drew back in a grin.

"Another truck comes in Monday. It might take longer but don't worry."

Arkady said nothing.

Kopf began walking away, then turned back.

"I forgot," he said, slowly drawing an envelope from his back pocket and laying it on the table.

Arkady turned the radio to WQXR. There was a special program on Jussie Björling, the Swedish tenor.

But something in the music bothered him. How was it possible to sing like that about love? Nobody loved. Pamina was a liar, Tamino a whore. Everyone lied. Hadn't war taught him that?

He switched off the radio, watched his breath plume and dissipate. Christmas, season of reproaches. He opened a drawer, drew out a copy of *Rogue,* flipped the pages, gazing at the girls with their silicone breasts and cherry-gum smiles. He slapped it down and stared at the parking lot and beyond it, to the airport. He rolled a toothpick over the back of the middle finger of his right hand, snapped it. He'd never been on a plane. Would it scare him? Maybe. He was growing old. No longer the young lion who impressed Stefan with his power, Lastivka with his wisdom.

Kopf didn't scare him; Kopf was nothing.

He picked up the *Journal.*

Fucking Kopf. Fucking Germans. The Germans hated Ukrainians. If Hitler had treated the Ukrainians squarely, he might have won the war.

He couldn't concentrate, fingered the envelope. Light. What was in it? How much?

Two hundred-dollar bills.

Incredible.

He'd figured maybe twenty, maybe fifty.

A week's pay.

He pushed back his blue cap.

The things he could do with this kind of cash. During the war everyone took bribes. He himself sold salversan to syphilitic Russians so he could buy meat on the black market. Who cared? The only difference between then and now was the war, which gave a man excuses, but life was life. God understood hunger and need. God knew who was to blame.

Why did he feel so unhappy?

"Hey, kid!"

Billy Whelan. Smiling Billy. He'd had a heart attack last year. He came back to work several months later unchanged. Arkady had met his wife at Oscar Landish's funeral. Big bones, frosted hair. He couldn't understand Billy's fast talk, his constant jokes, his steady humor.

The man acted as though the world was alright just as it was. Anyone needed help with the forklift or wanted time off—Billy was there. Like Arkady, he worked seven days a week, yet he was nearly sixty.

"You want anything from the cafeteria?" Billy beamed. "I'm off in an hour. For two weeks."

"What are you gonna do?"

"Florida. Sit on the beach, drink screwdrivers. Rent a boat, go out, you know, way out, maybe come back with a marlin."

Arkady smiled. But even with Billy he maintained a distance.

Alone again, he peered into the envelope. The two bills looked unreal. This kind of money, he could send Bo to Catholic school, pay off the car, the house.

All week he couldn't sleep. He listened to Stefan pacing overhead—Stefan himself rarely slept these days. He listened to the planes purring over Free Fall, imagined what it might feel like to jump from one in a parachute. What if he landed on an island, floating in a river, and no one saw him, how good it would be to begin again. He got up. Peeing, he stared stupidly out the window at the lilac shivering near the garage. Back in bed, he listened to the mulberry rapping the window, to Lastivka talking to herself in the next room above the hum of the new (and expensive) oil furnace.

Friday night he was in the booth reading the *Journal,* St. Matthew's Passion echoing off the glass.

When the truck drove up, he kept his eyes fixed to the paper.

After a second blast, the door opened. Footsteps. Fist rapping the window.

He looked up calmly.

The head facing him was huge and completely hairless. No eyebrows even. A splayed nose, lips fat as tires. Black leather jacket.

"Can I help you?"

"What? Open the fucking door, that's what."

More footsteps. Another plane.

"Open the fucking gate, man."

"What's the story, Mike?"

The little man on the other side of the glass stared at Arkady while talking to his partner. "Fuckin' guy's a pussy. I told you this guy was a pussy."

"Yeah. The man is makin' a statement. You makin' a statement?"

Arkady stayed silent.

"Yeah, let me say something to his face."

"No. We got friends here. Our friends will deal, be cool. One more time. You openin' that gate or not? Yes or no? I got things to do."

"Come on, Mike."

The next afternoon Arkady arrived at the booth to find someone else already there.

"What's the story?" he asked.

"Ask Kopf."

Kopf was on the phone, steel-toed Timberlands on the oak desk. When he saw Arkady, he hung up, rose, leaned forward, went to the door, kicked it shut.

He circled Arkady.

"Your booth, asshole. That's why you're here? Dumb Polack motherfucker. You think that's your booth. You think you own something here. Sure. Right. Ain't nothing, you hear me, nothing here that's yours. This is bullshit, man. What you did was bullshit. That shouldn't surprise me. You're shit. Everybody knows. Nobody, man, you are nobody.

"One more thing. You ever see me coming, take off. Just take off, man. You know I hate steppin' in shit. Hear me, dumb Polack motherfucker?"

"I'm not Polish," Arkady replied.

Several times during the war he'd come close to killing a man.

He balled his fists, buried them in his coat pockets.

He thought of his wife and son. He couldn't go home. He turned his back on Kopf and walked out the door.

Silver planes pierced the blue afternoon sky.

He loved the smell of the Chrysler's gray upholstery. He vacuumed it weekly, sponging the glossy black mats on the floor, wiping the windows.

The tank was full. He had money in his wallet.

The world was his. He was free. He could go anywhere. For years he'd traveled up 22, to the plant, back. But the world was a maze of routes. Maybe escape was possible.

In the car no one argued with him, no one told him what to do, no one screamed. He turned the key. Route 1 to Route 22, then the Parkway. Three lanes, each a freedom trail. He rolled down his window. Cool air swept in. He sang, "Oy die dunai, Oy die dunai, Oy die dunai danna." A nonsense song.

Newark, Elizabeth, Kenilworth, Linden, Rahway, Metuchen. North Jersey slipping past. The world was his desire. Wind riffled his hair. Glass smudged with the lipstick of insects.

Across the divider, cars, carrying the other dreamers, streaked past. He was riding the sky, he felt it, heading south. He'd always wanted to. Palm trees, exotic birds, perpetual sun. No matter that this was New Jersey. Dreams long drowned buoyed up with new life in a way he'd not let them since before the war.

The radio was busted so he kept singing. Ahead lay pines, rivers brimming with trout, a secret world of shiny mosses wrapping silver rocks below spruce. The parallel life: always there, waiting. No matter how you wasted yourself, what you did, there was always that other room, where life was also happening, and you were expected.

He knew now why he'd left his country: to drive wildly down the Parkway to freedom. Wasn't that the meaning of America? Highways opening to roads winding to towns edging highways — boundless desire met for once with a land great enough to satisfy it?

He'd rediscover the place. What was this talk about an empire in decline? He'd show the journalists, intellectuals, and spent emigré dreamers, worrying about morals and right living and responsibility. He'd cruise the highways like the new Columbus, sleeping in the car or under the stars or in motels if he had the cash. Maybe he wouldn't sleep at all. A lust for pure seeing, the longing to love a thing wholly, uncritically, fed him.

He waved, smiling to himself, at the horde of cars. The exodus from Egypt.

To be an enemy of busy-ness: that would be his role.

Wasn't that what he believed, even if he kept it to himself, kept it secret his whole life?

The big thoughts, finally. They too had been waiting.

He never wanted respectability or honor. Good God, he never wanted to be a grown man. Not in the world's way.

Onward and upward, to the cities of birds and all unfettered creatures. He'd live like the beatniks. Or he'd become like Skovoroda, the philosopher, who walked from village to village collecting folk songs.

He remembered his dreams of playing the piano in Harlem.

At Tom's River he turned onto Route 9. The hastening twilight chastened his fantasies. He grew hungry. He passed rest stops and restaurants but why waste a dollar on food that in a supermarket cost a quarter? He should have packed dinner.

His mouth was dry, his tongue a slab of salt.

Somewhere he'd gotten off the highway. Trees lined the shoulders. Insects splatted like grapes on the glass. He drove in the dark, headlights drilling the road. He braked for a coon. The darkness brimmed with impossible worlds. He rolled up his window. A yawn became a sigh. Why was he sighing? Wasn't he free, king of the road?

He stopped at a light. At the corner a new bank and on the hill above it a milky clapboard Presbyterian Church. Even in the dark the shops along Main Street glowed seductively—a florist, an auto parts store, a Kresge's. Across from them, a VFW and a mini-mart and something he couldn't see. At his corner a bar with the neon sign reading AVER.

136

He was thirsty.

Two motorcycles loomed up from the lot behind the bar, the bikers' long hair flapping behind them. They leaned into the road and tore up the hill.

Arkady considered running the light. Everything felt far away. The street lamps hummed like spaceships. They flickered like candles. Someone just died, he thought, and that flicker is all. His death would be like that, a snap of the fingers. No one to hear.

Now that he'd left everyone behind.

The light changed, but the feeling didn't, the taste of strangeness acrid on the back of the tongue, his skin prickling with uneasiness and curiosity. It was his right. He could go to any bar he wanted. So what if they didn't want him? So what? He could drink alone, bothering no one. As soon as he opened his mouth they'd know. They'd laugh. Even if nobody laughed, it would be as though everyone in the bar had shifted one stool over. That one stool shaped a chasm wide as the ocean.

The road climbed, unrolling velvety blackness, the sky now crosshatched with stars.

No one in the world ever gave him a thing. The world just took and took. His parents, his home. And in return? He hunched over the wheel, swallowed air as if it might cure the pain. He wanted a beer, signaled a U-turn, drove back to the bar.

Inside the smoky tavern a jukebox welcomed him with a wail.

The men at the bar sat absorbed by the TV. Others, scattered in pairs around tables, spoke softly. There were no women in the room.

A bearded man limped spryly round a pool table

while his opponent, a kid wearing a T-shirt and a leather jacket, leaned against a beam, sucking a smoke.

Arkady settled at the bar.

The albino bartender pressed his elbows into the stained oak and inclined his head in Arkady's direction.

"Pabst."

Wallpaper mallards, orange with smoke and time, drifted along the walls. A moose head grinned from a crossbeam.

The shabbiness disturbed him. He wasn't used to bars. During the war he entered taverns only to do black market business. He had no respect for men who hid in booze. Yet these men were laughing, relaxed.

He drained the glass, called for another and a box of pretzels.

"Fifteen cents."

He put down a quarter.

"You mind pennies, pal? I'm short. Didn't get to the bank. Crazy day."

The bartender wanted to talk. But Arkady couldn't, didn't think he had the words, so he nodded and counted the coins.

A voice behind him said, "That your Chrysler?"

Arkady tightened up, turned. He knew there would be trouble. The man had a doughy face, belly draped over his belt. Arkady never felt physical fear. "That's mine."

"You left your lights on . . . "

He nodded thanks. He finished his beer, rubbed his palm over the moist glass, dropped a few nickels, and pocketed the pretzels.

He was free.

Mist gleamed in the high beams, and he switched on the wipers. He was near the pine barrens, land flat and scrubby. A billion stars watched the black, empty roads, the darkness a cup gathering his thoughts, the usual ones assuring him he had no friends, and the only thing waiting for him were bills, mortgage, dentist, and car payments. God, even the car he drove wasn't his. It belonged to the Ukrainian Credit Union. He glared at the dark. Everyone conspired to keep him back, hold him down, trapped and sweating. Had anyone ever done a thing for him in his life? Just for him? His youth passed underground in bomb shelters and camps. He had no idea what life had to offer. He spent his middle years sweating for his family, but now his time had come. He was driving to freedom.

The smell of the ocean seeped in. He'd never been to Cape May before.

The grass hadn't been cut in weeks. Stefan was too old. Arkady hadn't seen his parents since he was a boy. He didn't even know where his mother was buried. And his father had been shot when the word *kulak* took on a new meaning. He remembered playing with toy soldiers in the back yard of his father's house while his father fed the chickens. The next day the lead soldiers had grown into real ones.

The road turned and he sped into the curve.

Fucking Kopf.

One by one the faces floated before him: Lastivka, Bo, Stefan. Then they appeared together, billeted around the dining room table. All wept.

When he died, no one would hear. No one would know. Only a flicker of the lamp.

He passed Victorian homes built when Cape May was still a haven for the Rockefellers and Duponts and Roosevelts. He saw boats on trailers in driveways. A dog raced out to the car.

He had no idea where he was. He turned right, and then the street came to an end.

The ocean.

His back ached. He'd been on the road for hours. He got out and walked to the top of the dune, from where he saw the Atlantic glimmering in the quarter-moonlight while clouds, stark and long as muscles, flexed across the sky. There were no gulls, an occasional foghorn far away. Waves broke on the shore with a woosh and pulled back, dragging out the weight of his rage. The wind blew hard and he zipped his coat. The sea's relentless tumbling calmed him.

The flicker of a street lamp. And life would go on.

That was why he had to go back. Who was he? What was a life without witnesses? He would flicker and go out. Without his family, the little he had would turn to nothing. He should never have left. Never have left the farm, the old country, Free Fall. The undertow held him, pulled him down. He was at the mercy of great powers, but they couldn't get all of him. He had a heart: it had its own drama. His history was his wife, his son, his family. Even if he and Lastivka couldn't work things out, at least with her he knew who he was. He was above all a creature of feeling. His ferocity faded. Even if he had spoiled his life, he could show the world he had the character to stick by his choices.

He walked to the edge of the water. The sea, breaking, seemed to say: Speak, you are heard. The waves tumbled through him, washing him clean with their cold and their salt, as though something in him had needed to hear them before he could hear himself, and the wind, while he stood at the end of this long blind alley in his world, cold and clean, blew new air into his lungs.

Last Loves

AFTER LYING in bed reading the Bible and yesterday's paper, Stefan showered. He breakfasted on bread covered with honey. Afterwards he swept the crusts into the newspaper and stuffed the parcel into his coat pocket. He walked down North Burdock to the river.

His cane clicked against the sidewalk. From the blue house fronted by Doric columns came the sound of a polonaise, and the notes tangled with the random xylophone of the sparrows. A woman prodding a stroller walked by. She smiled and Stefan flexed the brim of his fedora.

In the park he sat on a bench near the dam. The sound of the water helped him to think clearly. Caprices of light bobbed on the waves as though they too heard the music.

Time whirled like a music box ballerina. He'd walked under bridges by the Seine, past campfires around which families huddled. He pulled the paper from his pocket and scattered the crusts over the grass. Most of the ducks had already left. He had walked down the Rue de Descartes talking about Picasso and the surrealists. Snows of etcetera. *Never married, never harried.* And his great projects? Mere notes — leaves awaiting the match. When he wasn't at Woolworth's, he occasionally visited the Shevchenko Scientific Society on Second Avenue, where he studied documents, made outlines. But he lacked primary sources. Once, in the reading room of the library on Forty-second Street, he ran into his old acquaintance Dr. Zahajkewicz: this former colleague of his brother's now worked as a cook in a Spanish restaurant in Harlem. Stefan told him about Woolworth's and Claudia, the young Italian girl. She might as well have been Polynesian for all the names D'Annunzio or Montale or Pavese meant to her.

Sitting in the park, Stefan smiled over their flirtation. She'd complained to him about blacks moving into her neighborhood, about her mother, who wouldn't let her wear makeup. "Why dabble with a finished work of art?" he'd asked.

The manager at Woolworth's was a twenty-four-year-old Polish kid who knew nothing about the history of relations between Ukraine and Poland. America. Sweet amnesia.

On quiet days in the store, Stefan stared for hours at the goldfish or the gerbils whirling in their metal wheels. And I'm no different, he thought.

He took a little book from his pocket. An illustrated life of the painter George Rouault. Stefan had met him once. The great artist had leaned over to him and said how he hated that under their bright facades the middle class really *were* happy. So French. At the time he hadn't liked Rouault's paintings. Now the impasto clowns seemed thick with meaning. He studied a pastel cemetery with clouds like fish in a blue-green sky. The crosses marking the graves appeared to be *X*'s marking the site of a treasure.

He didn't hear Gwen McDonald clomping down the macadam path.

"Why, Mr. Zabobon, isn't it glorious? Oh, a book!"

Stefan rose and hooded his heart with his hat.

"My good Mrs. McDonald. Yes, a book."

"Well, and of all people, Root. How coincidental. I'm on my way to an opening at the gallery. A special event for seniors. Have you heard that phrase, 'senior citizens'?"

They walked arm in arm over the bridge. Big-boned Gwen, with thick gray hair. And many virtues. She was patient with his accent. In her company, he always groomed his sentences.

"Have you heard about the shelter? The president thinks the Russians might attack. They're all over town. Do you know where? In the basements of schools and homes. It's ridiculous. They're planning drills. They tell the children to put their heads down on the desk. For an atom bomb. Do you think it will make a difference? Would the Russians do something like that?"

He raked his cane against the fieldstone wall. She forced him to rethink his ideas about beauty. The curve of a nose, the crest of a cheekbone, the plumpness of breasts. Gwen McDonald owned none of these things that once lured him to seek the tuck and comfort of flesh. Yet he felt the sad animal stir and longed to rest his head on her shoulder. His old heart opened. He wanted to draw everything down into himself. Desire. Women! It was his brother, that religious man, who'd suffered the most for them. First Zenon had scuttled his career for Natalka, then his life for his mistress.

He himself had also followed his appetites. As a result, there were things he'd missed out on: he'd never know the pleasure of long-standing intimacy. Yet his bachelorhood kept him alert; his loneliness he blew away with Plato, chess, and the unfiltered eroticism of Rubens and Ingres. He read the *Symposium* and wondered if he'd ever met a Diotima without recognizing her. Maybe men really did aim for the good—but he was too worldly, too thick in the woods to see clearly. Nevertheless, the sweetness of the day absorbed him.

"Something wrong, Mr. Zabobon?" Her question.

"The Russians may be family to Genghis Khan, but I don't think it's up to them. It's the machines themselves. They'll decide what happens."

At the moment the prospect of the end of the world worried him less than the idea that he had wasted his life.

Wind slurred dreamily through the maples.

He respected the impulse to art more than anything. The local Picasso wore gravy-colored turtlenecks and had his pupils painting green circles and triangles. They worked with fluorescent colors. In art, though, standards were essentials. On the religious plane, the fellow's portraits were valuable as Da Vinci's. As art, they were crap.

"And may we expect to see Mr. Parkinson's works in this exhibition?"

"Absolutely."

He drifted again. He couldn't connect with the moment. Not even with the sensual occasion. He decided to keep talking.

"Mrs. McDonald, have you ever thought that the stones and trees and even the water want to speak? I think the only difference between us and objects is that we have words to give another life to the things that contain us. Birds and fish don't need words to become themselves. We do. We're made by the language we hear. Sorry, the wind blows these strange thoughts in. You're kind to listen. I come from a place where the earth has been trying to speak for so long, I'm afraid when it finally does, the first thing it will do is scream.

"I know I have no place in America. I came here to die. Here I'm good for guarding goldfish. A satisfying occupation, I assure you. I'm not complaining. I'm not unhappy. The opposite, really. But what . . . ah, but here we are, at the library . . . "

"And there's Mr. Parkinson. Yoo-hoo! Frank!"

Avon Calling

LASTIVKA WANTED to feel again the joy she'd known as a girl racing around the cemeteries of a city which must have existed only in dreams.

Painting her eyes and lips, she looked in the mirror. Where had those lines come from?

"Mother, did you know father's father? Mother, tell me how father was shot."

Natalka sat still as a Buddha in her chair. "Do you remember Eddie doing handstands in the pantry, mother?"

Lastivka missed the sense of purpose the war had given them. Arkady's forced sing-alongs weren't enough. She needed a mission.

"Father, how should we educate the boy?"

Zenon dragged on his pipe a minute. "Better teach him about home. He may prove useful. May be needed later."

"What is it like among the dead?"

"Not bad, angel. Nothing like what we at the Near-Death Society thought it might be. I've been to California. I've been to the Metropolitan. It's hard to explain. Some of us get to go wherever we want to. Others have restrictions. You should see the crowds in Marilyn Monroe's bedroom at night. Me, I visit Rozdorizha. I keep looking for Toor. No sign yet. But he's been dead a long time. The things he knows!"

"Why don't you talk to mother? She needs you."

Zenon smiled. "We're in constant communication, your mother and I. We're never out of touch. In fact, she spends a lot more of her time with me than she does with you. I know you think she's lost most of her mind. It's not true, darling. She spends a lot of time with me."

"Are the priests right?"

"It's much more complicted than what they can say. So many of them have pedestrian imaginations. They have fetishes. They're fixed on a couple of colors, blue and red and gold. They've got a few details, like wings —I won't deny it. But that's such a tiny part of it. What can men know about the imagination of God? Not even the dead understand it."

One morning Lastivka awoke with the word *Paris* in her head.

She went into Bo's room and sat down on the edge of his bed.

She shook his shoulder until he woke up.

"Better pack. We're going to Paris soon."

She then walked over to his blue and yellow dresser and began taking his clothes out. She piled them on his blue and yellow quilt on the bed.

"Mother," he said, a little frightened. "Why? Why are we going to Paris?"

150

"Because it's the center of beauty and culture," she said, surprised by the question.

"All right," he sighed, rubbing his eyes. At least he didn't have to do push-ups. He wasn't convinced. But he wasn't going to argue, either. This too might prove a source of pleasure, like the chocolates from Macy's.

Paris might be just the place to build a monument to his mother. This was something to which he'd given serious thought. Who else in the world was as concerned as she was with satisfying his desires?

Lastivka kept folding clothes.

The pile grew and grew.

"Can I take my soldiers?"

"No," she suddenly snapped.

"Why not?"

"They're too heavy."

"Mother, that's silly."

"I don't care. You can't take the soldiers. No more soldiers."

This was a serious problem. Bo brooded. But he was sure it would be a mistake to resist her.

She was struggling to close one of the suitcases when Stefan, back from work, peered in.

"And where are we off to?"

"Things don't happen that way," Arkady said to her later. "Things don't happen just because you want them to."

Now it was Paris. This strange woman. Sometimes he feared she'd lose touch completely, like her mother.

"You have to work for things. Step by step. You have to make plans and stick with them."

Lastivka shut her eyes. She thought of what her father said about the imagination of God. If there were people with wings, and crowds of the dead spied on the living, then going to Paris was a tiny matter in the scheme of things, and God could settle it in a wink. Surely Paris was nothing. Millions went each day.

"I know why you want to go to Paris," Arkady said, more softly. "I do."

She looked at him, her eyes doubtful. He grasped so little. Could he possibly understand this?

"It's because you can't go home. I know." Then he turned to his son. "Show your mother how beautifully you do push-ups."

Lastivka kept talking about Paris and finally Arkady agreed that he would split the plane fare with her. But first she had to get a job to earn her share.

At the seminar the woman gave her a pink molded plastic sample case, a box of catalogs, and a stack of order forms. She was now an Avon lady.

"It's all in the attitude," said the instructor, an aggressively cheerful woman with frosted hair, false pearls, and lipstick smeared on like an open wound.

The instructor kept saying over and over how you had to remember that you were giving people something they really wanted. But Lastivka saw herself lifting the customer by the scruff of the neck, like a stunned rabbit, and dropping her in a burlap sack. That was business. And as to attitude — what a wild superstitious notion that was!

But this was the only road to Paris, and if she had to, she would walk it.

She made her first sales, five dollars in one afternoon, to friends in the Society of Ukrainian Women, which met once a month in the church hall in Elizabeth.

Gradually she worked her way over to Free Fall.

One morning, Mrs. Roberts, whom Lastivka knew as the head of the PTA, opened the door.

Lastivka flushed.

She explained her mission.

"Oh, I could use some cologne for Ben. Come in."

She beckoned Lastivka into the foyer.

She had just closed the door when the bell rang again.

"Excuse me. Oh, Angela, I was just saying to . . . I'm sorry, I realize I don't know your name. Vorog? How unusual. I was just — oh, never mind. Come with me, Angela. Will you excuse me a minute?"

Mrs. Roberts and the cleaning woman walked down the hall.

Persistence. That was another word the woman at the seminar had used. Get in the door and you get the sale. That was the rule. Get the sale and you get the commission. That was the goal. Get the commission and you get Paris.

She brushed her hair down with long nervous fingers which hadn't touched a piano in years except to play the national anthem. Looking in the Venetian mirror, she noticed she wasn't wearing any makeup. The lady had said repeatedly that a salesgirl was her own best ad.

Remember: the products *sell themselves.* They had already sold themselves to millions. All you had to do was show them.

Lastivka stared skeptically at the tiny sample tubes and bottles. Were they really that powerful? Could she put all her faith in them? She pulled out a catalog and turned to the men's colognes. Would Arkady like one of the Model Ts? A dumbbell?

"Who are you?" A girl, about seven, in pigtails, stood a few feet away, hugging a stuffed skunk to her breast.

"Is that the Avon lady, Sadie?" the girl asked the black woman walking down the hall.

"Don't call me Sadie, child. Excuse me, ma'am. Mrs. Roberts just had a call. She'll be out momently."

Lastivka stared at the peacocks strutting across the rug under her feet. What if she began babbling in Ukrainian?

She was practicing her patter to the mirror when Mrs. Roberts returned. Caught. Lastivka blushed. She jerked her arm to point to the many fine products in the case. Case and arm met. Sixty-eight tubes of lipstick and a dozen bottles of perfume bounced off the peacocks.

She crouched, mumbling apologies in every language she knew. In French, German, Rumanian, Polish, and Czech.

Mrs. Roberts smiled tightly.

Lastivka rose, tubes in hand, cleared her throat, and smiled at her customer.

"What kind of name is that?" Mrs. Roberts asked.

" 'Heart Robber,' " Lastivka said, staring at the tube in her hand.

"No. Vorog. I mean Vorog. You said that was your name."

"Oh. Ukrainian. It's Ukrainian."

"I don't think I've ever met a Ukrainian. Isn't that like Russian?"

She had arrived in Klagenfurt with Stefan near Easter. That Easter Sunday not a single church bell rang. Her father had stayed home to settle some business. Then they got the telegram from a young boy with sniffles. The note had been sent by a friend. It said Zenon had been shot. It was a long time before she found out why.

"No," she said to Mrs. Roberts. "No."

She didn't feel like explaining the difference. Instead, she opened the catalog to the page offering men's cologne.

Mrs. Roberts chose "Body Buddy." Lastivka wrote up the order while from another room she heard the little girl shout, "No, no, no, Sadie. I said no, no, no."

As she opened the door, Mrs. Roberts asked, "Do you ever get homesick?"

The question distressed her. It's the world, she thought. It won't let things be. Always reminding us we're not at home here.

Before she could speak, Mrs. Roberts broke in gently. "What a stupid question. Of course you do. Why, I get homesick after a week in Hawaii. That's where Ben and I go for Christmas. Or did until Natalie was born . . . "

Lastivka felt humiliated. She couldn't even sell makeup. Look at Mrs. Roberts. There was a woman. She stood in the world proudly. She was what life could make of people if it were so inclined. What was the use of all her feelings? There was nothing she could do with them.

She went home by way of the cemetery.

"Father," she called softly. But he did not appear.

Lastivka came home to find the usual entourage scattered around her living room. Even her mother was there, in her wooden wheelchair, wearing a blue striped dress and gnawing a candied apple.

Everyone seemed especially excited.

"My friends, we've reached a crossroad!" cried the colonel from his perch atop the sofa.

Around him his audience of sympathizers stood open-mouthed and closed-fisted.

"My theory is that every theory is born of a man's physical and psychological constitution . . . "

"You're a materialist!"

"Americans love conspiracy theories. Bilderbergers, trilateralists, Masons. These organizations are part of the folklore. It comes from the government being so big. At any moment only a fraction of the population is near the center of power, though the center itself is surprisingly mobile."

The talk, informed by ignorance yet humanly necessary, echoed through the apartment.

Adriana Benko had brought her reducing machine: a vibrating vinyl bed. Lastivka had hoped to get her mother to try it. Instead, Uncle George, one of the twins, strapped himself down, while Pavlo stood over him, whistling "Row Row Row Your Boat." The machine hummed like a cast-iron mosquito.

Stefan leaned on his cane in the doorway. He was worried. Arkady was not in the room. And the crowd seemed thirsty for blood.

"We must show the Americans we're here!"

Lastivka tried to understand what was going on.

"We have suffered much in our long and tragic history! Yet never has our dignity been so . . . " Words failed him.

"What happened?" she asked Stefan.

"Sam's boss at the hospital slapped her!"

"But she's not here."

"That's true. She and Edward went up to the Catskills."

"Then what are they doing?"

Stefan looked at his niece. Did he really need to explain?

"Arms, we need arms," Adriana shouted, rubbing Pavlo's thigh.

She'd mistaken him for George.

Puzzled, Pavlo pushed her away.

Flashing an angry look, she leapt to the couch next to the colonel and raised her fists the way she had seen the blacks do on television.

"I have two of them!"

George laughed.

"Turn that machine off or I'll punch your nose!" the colonel ordered.

"There are knives in the kitchen!"

"They will do, they will do."

"*Allons enfants de la patrie*," Adriana sang.

There are times when madness is called for, when humankind cannot respond with less. Times it needs Christians chewed by lions, Jews in the ovens, Armenians diced. One sees it in the classics: Agamemnon, Lysistrata. And in the religions, too: Christ on the cross, Buddha forty days under the Bo tree, martyrs flayed.

Be it noted that in the course of the rally, while the colonel stomped and perorated and Adriana sang, at least three bottles of good cheap whiskey and a quart of vodka took the short way to the trash barrel.

The fuming crowd began moving down the stairs.

"Take me with you, take me with you." It was Natalka, who'd hardly spoken in a decade. She held the stick in her hand.

"Yes, let's carry her."

"She can walk."

"I can walk."

And Natalka, who never walked anymore, got out of her wooden wheelchair and headed toward the stairs. The crowd stared in awe.

They broke into applause.

At the head of the stairs, Natalka turned to her supporters. "For Zenon," she said, before slumping down.

Her large soft body folded and opened like an accordion on its way down the stairs. It stopped at the door which, at that moment, Arkady opened.

The ambulance arrived too late. Within the hour Lastivka was told by a young Korean doctor at Overlook Hospital in Summit that her mother was dead.

It was not the first time a revolution ended in a funeral.

The Carpathians

ADRIANA BENKO told Lastivka about a Ukrainian resort in the Catskills called the Carpathians.

Saturday, just as they were getting ready to leave, Bo got a stomachache. And what about the dog?

When Bo whimpered he wanted Brovko along, Lastivka said, "Darka will be there." Darka was his cousin.

"So?"

"You'll have plenty of company. Father will take care of the dog."

Arkady had to work. He would visit them on weekends.

Green fields flickered, horses grazed, people with backpacks and walking sticks hiked along the side of the road. A hand-lettered sign said *Raspberries: Pick Your Own.* They drove by vegetable and fruit stands, as well as one flatbed pickup piled with old shoes peddled by a man wearing a bright orange shirt and a cowboy hat. The long shadows of trees played on the freshly oiled gravel. Finally they turned down a dirt drive, cruised past a sign half hidden by red maples which said *Carpathians* and through a tunnel of trees, past the clay tennis court where grass and mullein and goldenrod were knee-high.

Half a dozen bungalows lined each side of a close-cropped field humming with grasshoppers and crickets and cicadas. In the center stood a flagpole onto which each dawn Mr. Holowniski, proprietor, hoisted the Ukrainian flag, while the anthem blared from a single speaker braced to a tree. All day music poured from it: Borodin's *Polovtsian Dances*, arias by Mario Lanza, favorites from Mitch Miller and the Gang. A barn near the pond housed a ping-pong table, a piano with no middle C, a yellowed wicker sofa, and musty-cushioned chairs. Lastivka saw her cousin Edward Zaremba standing beside the barn door, drinks in both hands.

Pear-shaped Edward, their downstairs neighbor in Free Fall, had not been sober for quite a few years. It was a choice he'd made. During the war Edward had decided that nothing, not poverty nor failure, would unhinge him. What good had money or social position done the Jews of Rozdorizha? No, it was a fool's game. How had their important positions helped the city's judges and the lawyers? How had it helped his parents, both of whom had been shot by the Bolsheviks? Only the stupid and the innocent worried about money or prestige. Death was everywhere, waiting around the corner, always. He couldn't hold a job (though it was Edward who'd gotten Arkady into the SeaLand Plant). He drifted. He drove cabs, unloaded trucks at the local supermarket, swept the train station in Free Fall. It didn't matter. Or he made you believe it didn't. His wife and his daughter too seemed to have accepted his terms. He was always smiling, drink in hand.

Coming out of the door behind him was Halka, and waving a straw hat, Adriana . . .

Lastivka's heart opened: she was among friends. Here she did not need the wigs. Here, for two weeks a year, she felt entirely safe. Without the daily arguments that marked domestic life in Free Fall, her spirits bloomed. She cooked earnestly. She read. Some evenings she read aloud from the most recent emigré journals.

Wasps nested under the eaves of the Vorog bungalow. One night Bo woke to a bat thumping about the room. How did it get in when the door and window were closed? He opened the window and waited while it knocked into the mirror, thrashed around the slicker hanging from the door, and finally dropped back out into the night. He sat at the sill, listening to the loon.

After breakfast, he set out with Stefan down the path hidden by the willow on the far side of the pond at the edge of the woods. It was narrow and they walked single file, Stefan five feet ahead, wagging his cane.

"That's a pearly everlasting, that's a turtle's head, and that pretty little thing that looks like an orchid, that's a touch-me-not. A *noli-me-tangere*, as we say in Latin. I've known girls like that. Seriously, child, you know where that comes from? Our Lord and Savior Jesus Christ said that when someone tried to touch him when he walked through a crowd. He said some of his virtue had left him. Or maybe I'm getting it wrong."

"Why were people trying to touch him?"

"Because he was so good."

"Like the Beatles."

"Who?"

"On the radio." No one in his house ever knew what he was talking about.

"America. We'll never keep up with you. What are they teaching you in school?"

"Pencil sharpening."

"Good thing." He didn't miss a beat. "Soon you won't want to use the ones I whittle down with my poor razor. Next year you should take Latin."

"Uncle, if I want to, but not until the eighth grade."

"Yes, but by then you should want to."

"A naked lady is called a dude."

"This is what they're teaching?"

Peepers croaked in ponds barely visible through the bushes. Seeing a place like that, Stefan told him, added years to your life. Because, he explained, we are nourished by our eyes as much as by our stomachs.

Light cut a path straight through the trees, with forest shadowing them on both sides. Farther in lay pines and birches, toppled by lightning or rot. Bo remembered Stefan's stories about Toor, who sat on the apple trees as though they were chairs.

Webs tickled his cheeks as he passed through an archway of wild roses. The flower, when he peered in, was red and shiny and wet as a newly washed apple. Billions of midges, mosquitoes, imperious dragonflies. He felt as though something just below or just above his skin wanted to break free.

They passed a meadow where the grass was flecked with flakes of mirror, as though it had rained here and nowhere else.

At the top of the slope towered an oak shaped like an upside down J. A wooden swing hung from the hook.

"Sit," Stefan commanded.

He rested his cane and gave Bo a push, and he flew into the sun like a ball with a string attached.

After a while they plunged back. It was hard keeping pace with Stefan, who reminded Bo of a fox, snout thrust forward, lean body probing the air.

Out of the woods emerged the strangest house, of white stone with a straw roof and sunflowers bobbing around like sentries.

In the doorway stood an old man dressed in white. White pants and white shirt hanging down to his knees like a skirt. His white beard parted and from it poked a tiny gray head with small shoulders: a squirrel wriggled down to his chest, and dropped to the ground.

"Who's the boy?"

Stefan introduced him to Semenko, the beekeeper.

"You're tiny," he said.

Bo stared at the squirrel nibbling sunflower seeds. In the one-room house stood a long pine table surrounded by four chairs and in the corner, a cot. The guests sat at the table while the beekeeper fussed in the kitchen. He gave them each a plate on which lay wax honeycombs oozing gold. Bo felt it was like church.

The old man recited a quick prayer. "Eat!" he said, laughing.

Bo bit down, chewing wax and all. The wax tasted warm and strange. He wiped his lips with the back of his hand and no one minded.

The men talked and he left the table and paced around the house. Outside a hive perched on sticks. The bees ignored him, flying among the crab apples and swooping low for the tiny white flowers. He followed the squirrel as it rooted among the leaves.

The world hovered near his eyes. For the first time he was seeing things as they really were.

Stefan came out when the sun was blazing lower in the sky, and they returned by the same path, but Bo didn't recognize anything. In a matter of hours all had changed.

Walking, Stefan felt the old world burning away like mist. All those women—sweat with sweat, kisses, lips—fading, and the only reason any of it happened was so that he could keep alive a few names and memories, pass something on.

Evenings everyone gathered in the barn.

They came in formal attire: the women, perfumed, in long dresses; the men in ties. They came to sing, argue, tell stories.

Judge Kaminsky said, "Did I ever tell you about the time I found myself in a cell with a rapist I'd sent to prison? A great story. I was a political prisoner, of course. Not a criminal. Servant of a different idea. But, sitting there with my rapist friend, politics and ideas didn't count. My mind was dark. My hands shook. You know what saved me? The rapist. After not saying anything for days, he came up to me and said, 'I know you. You're the man who sent me here. Sir.' And he walked away. Instead of trying to kill me, he sat in the corner saying his beads. I think he was saying his beads. Guilt did that to him."

"What we need," said Pavlo, "is a revolution. We need to start a revolution."

"What are you talking about? Didn't we try that once?" Adriana asked.

"Guilt," said Colonel Levko, pushing back his wire-rimmed glasses, sniffling, "is the dullest emotion in the world. Self-indulgence of petty men. Perfectly predictable. There are people who live too expansively when luck is with them. When it goes, they're all mea culpa and sorrow."

"Anybody for *stuk-puk?*" George asked.

"I disagree," countered the judge. "You can't hope to have a vital inner life without feeling, and surviving, guilt. It isn't pleasant but it's necessary. I can't tell you how many times I've lost sleep worrying over whether or not I'd made the right decision in a case. But I believe having a conscience makes me a better judge."

"Conscience!" snapped Colonel Levko. "Invented by man to torture himself and his younger brothers. I'm responsible for thousands of deaths. Doesn't bother me at all."

"You haven't had a good night's sleep in years, Levku. Everyone knows that."

"You don't understand anything. As usual. My insomnia is hereditary. My father was a light sleeper. So was my grandfather. And who needs it? Life is action. I may make mistakes, but I don't worry about that. Religion does this, you know. It makes you soft. Only cowards repent. I'll take my stand with the great Cunningham Grahame, who said, 'I'll never withdraw.'"

"Wonder how his wife felt . . . "

"Think of Napoleon and Ney at Friedland and Borodino!"

"Battle of Leipzig!"

"And why?"

Adriana confessed, "Why what? Oh dear, I'm confused."

"Naturally, Napoleon trusted the Hapsburgs. We know better. We lived under those damned Austrians. He believed his marriage to the emperor's daughter would give him the old man's infantry."

"What's all this about Napoleon? Let's discuss Khmelnitsky or Mazeppa . . . "

"Bila Tserkva!"

"You can't honor Napoleon and God . . . "

"Render unto to Caesar . . . "

"Yes, well and good. But that's the way to despair . . . "

"Napoleon did more for democracy than a million Kennedys . . . "

"You know he slept six hours? It didn't matter when. Hour here, hour there . . . "

"Khmelnitsky was a traitor . . . "

"You understand, my theory about war and love holds up. Think, a man like Napoleon cuckolded by both his wives! Josephine was a slut, and Marie-Thérèse lived openly with Neipperg!"

"You know he believed the most important thing for winning a war was morale. That's what we Ukrainians need . . . "

"Faith . . . "

"Character . . . "

166

"But it's impossible in the States. We're not Anglo-Saxon enough. We're different types."

"Yes, but here everyone fights his way in. The British and the French hated each other at first. The Puritans ran from torture and the Indians didn't exactly greet them with open arms. Everybody gets hell here. At first. You stick it out, that's all."

"What arrogance," the judge burst in, looping back to the conversation he'd had with the colonel minutes before. "You deny man his only chance for personal redemption!"

"Wrong. He's not arrogant. The opposite," Stefan interjected. "Don't you see that anyone who accepts a system, any system, Hegel's or Christ's or Marx's, says he's found Truth. The colonel is open-minded."

"You're making fun of me, Stefan."

Stefan shrugged.

"But that's you. You're a mocker. You mock everything. Have you ever told us what you believe? You stand outside everything. You don't care about God or country. I don't know a thing about God. He isn't real to me. But my country I understand."

"To hell with this," a voice from near the fireplace added: "Here's a toast to the plumbing, without which we'd all be up shit's creek."

"Tell us what you believe . . . "

"I believe," Stefan said, "in specific acts of kindness. No rhetoric about the general good. If you see a chance to help a man, do it and shut up. You atheists," he turned to Kaminsky, who was about to object, "in your muddled minds, crown the conscience then behead the king. By elevating the individual conscience, you create the conditions for a physics of morality. For every so-called evil action you oblige yourselves to perform a redemptive one. Transgression. Redemption. You waste your lives playing moral ping-pong. Or, in your case, Colonel, you overthrow conscience, behave self-indulgently, and gasp with excitement at your own power when no one punishes you. I believe in something entirely different . . . "

"The problem with the peasants," Pavlo said to Adriana — the couple had drifted out to the pine near the garage, "is they kept thinking of wealth exclusively in terms of land. They didn't understand capital."

She smiled. Leaned her hips into his. He moved to kiss her and pressed a palm to her heavy breast.

"Grace," said the judge, scratching his left ankle with his foot. "Ridiculous. You can't speak about a workable Christianity in this age. Impossible."

A few feet away from them, George did American imitations. He laughed heartily, slapped a back, pumped an imaginary hand.

Under the pine, near the garage, Adriana, skirt hiked above her hips, panties in pocket, moaned.

Stefan said, "You see me as a Christian in a nest of pagans. Strange." He wanted to believe it himself. "But your objection's dumb. Supercilious souls have always disbelieved. History can't imply universal progress away from God. God is, by definition, the permanent. Only names and disguises change. Just as truth isn't static or partisan. It shifts. It wants us wondering.

"The man who's found his soul, something immortal linked to the body, has won the most important battle of his life. Or, better, say, his life's just started."

"How is the soul different from the conscience?" asked the judge.

Stefan was about to answer when Lastivka announced that it was time for coffee and dessert. The crowd moved toward the Vorog bungalow.

"Come down, boy," Stefan called to Bo, who was wrapped like a possum round the roof beam.

From his vantage point the world's inhabitants looked tiny and pathetic. When he heard Stefan, he, in keeping with his personal convictions, stuck out his tongue.

"Boy, I'm too old to get up there with you. Come down, and I'll tell you a secret."

Bo hopped down. Standing beside the old man, he closed his eyes, clogged his ears with his fingers. Stefan knew this was his way of listening.

"Boy, life is a plain affair. It's hard to see this sometimes. One gets confused so easily. If you listened to these men below, you'd be lost in a week. But never let anyone tell you life isn't the simplest thing in the world. If one has one's eyes open. As for life's great secrets, the deeper mysteries . . . This much I can leave you. If you're ever bothered by some trivial affair, the fading of love, or a creditor's phone calls, tell yourself you possess one of the finer things, a great truth. You do, you know. You're sitting on it.

"Think about the acorn. As a start. Anything will do. Grain of sand. Anything. But think about the acorn for a few hours: where it comes from, and then the origins of that. Follow an idea to its end. I promise that if you think long enough and hard enough about a simple acorn, it will bloom into a tree of light, and you'll climb its trunk and rest yourself among the leaves and the branches of brightness, and you'll be able to stay there forever if you want to."

"Feed me," Bo said.

"Let's build a fire," Bo said to Darka.

It was twilight and the mosquitoes were starting to bite.

"Okay," his cousin agreed.

They gathered twigs and branches and carried them to the Indian Village. Soon the fire was throwing their shadows onto the trees.

Bo said, "Let's wrestle."

He stripped off his sweater. Darka kept her jacket on. They crouched. He bounced his knuckles against the grass and smiled eagerly. Darka shook her arms to loosen up. She sneezed, swiped her nose with the back of her hand. Bo jumped for her legs. He got her ankle, pulled it, and she fell, yelping, but the grass was thick and cushioned her. She was stunned and then he was on top, boring his shoulder into her belly, higher, rubbing her small breasts and then rolling over her. He rolled his palms up and down her belly and then again over her breasts, flattening them, though they were already tiny. Then his hand was on her thigh. He was turning her over, his wrist was between her legs. She yelped and moaned. His hand was on her fanny, lifting her legs up. His wrist pushed deeper down between her legs. She shut her eyes. She felt like smiling until a rock cut into her shoulder and she was jarred from her trance. She sat up, pushing the startled boy off, and then she swatted him a shut fist to the side of the head.

Both sat in the grass a few minutes.

Darka laughed.

"Bedtime," Lastivka called from the bungalow.

"I'll put the fire out," said Bo.

"It's already out."

"Look, sparks . . . "

"Come on, catch me . . . "

She ran and he looked over at the fire and then raced after the girl.

In the middle of the night he woke to screams. He pulled the sheet over his head.

But the screams were louder than usual.

He got up.

There were people in the field, and it was very bright, and he realized the tennis court was on fire, red and gold and white flames lashing the sky like lightning spouting up from the earth. He ran out. People rushed about with buckets and pots of water. He waved to Darka, but she didn't see him from the other side of the field.

He went to the flagpole and waited. Darka eventually

came over. "What will we do?" He looked at her. "What will we tell them?"

"They already know." She was crying.

Mr. Holowinsky ran two hoses from the barn, a third from the house. Luckily, earlier that day he'd been watering the peppers and tomatoes, and a hose was already hooked up.

There was a roar and they saw Mr. Holowinsky in the bulldozer, riding straight for the fire. He pushed a mound of dirt. Soon the field was framed by a wall of earth.

The sky was growing brighter when they went back to bed.

The next morning Lastivka seemed tenser than usual. "Time to pack," she said.

Her face was long and sad. Bo had noticed she was happiest right after talking to her father's ghost.

"Hurry, dear, bring your suitcase."

He lifted the small bag and walked into the hall, through the dining room. The day was heating up. The tennis field look black. He saw his mother at the car Arkady had brought near the bungalow.

His father sat at the table on the porch, an empty coffee cup on the orange place mat before him, the newspaper open. Looking up, he seemed not to recognize Bo. His eyes clouded.

Bo froze.

"You know how much that cost me? You know?"

"A lot of money, Father."

"More than you'll ever know." He bored into the paper. "Go help your mother."

Bo walked slowly by.

Safe, out of reach, when the chair behind him scraped the floor. Something landed heavily on the back of his neck, sending him forward, stumbling, to the ground.

Abu Dhabi

AROUND THANKSGIVING, which again passed un-
celebrated in the Vorog household, the insomniac
Stefan, who hadn't slept through a whole night in a decade, caught a cold.

"To bed," Dr. Hlib commanded, dragging on a Pall
Mall.

Stefan lay in the attic, frowning at Ingres's *Odalisque*.
He had wasted his life.

Above his head hung a wooden cross supporting a
carved Christ. One of the nails had come loose, and the
figure swerved from high noon to about one-forty.

A pine desk stood against the wall. It was riddled with
pigeon holes stuffed with envelopes, pencils, pipe clean-
ers, and packets of stamps. The bookcase held his albums, art books, volumes of history, and several ledgers
of notes for the projects he'd labored at unsuccessfully
over a lifetime, including his *Suggestions Toward a Prelimi-
nary Theory of Marriage* and his *History of Rozdorizha*.

A few white hairs meandered over his pate. His mustache and goatee were tightly pruned around a perpetu-
ally runny nose. His right eye glared directly ahead
while the left, rheumy, roved anarchically in its socket.

His knobby stockinged feet stuck out under the quilt like bulbs. And he had once been called Casanova.

He coughed, sneezed, and buried himself under a mound of Kleenex.

One morning, as Lastivka aimed a spoonful of pea soup toward his mouth, he exploded, "I don't want it!" The spoon fell, splattering the quilt with green.

He glared at the filigreed leaves of the ming aralia. Shame, shame. What kind of behavior was this? His lips clamped in a sulk. *Leave me be: it's not even noon. Sinners need long bouts of silence for reflection.*

Lastivka sat stiffly. She'd just returned from mass, reeking of the ciborium. The fanatic made a daily pilgrimage.

Drunkards.

No, he reminded himself. Not his place to judge. Religion was the science of feelings. People could always use a reminder of the historical triumph of charity over competition.

No, behave. You are the beneficiary of her devotional nature.

Her eyes clapped back tears.

Tears! Tears everywhere! Trying to drown him. She was made of sterner stuff, surely. *The war, think of the war. Children's bodies in the streets covered with flies.*

He felt like a shit. He recalled the first time he saw her. Occasionally, when he saw someone for the first time, his mind would generate an image of that person as a child. The cop clutched a cap gun; the albino behind the counter in the supermarket tugged her sister's braid; the bum in the park shrank, skin tightening, splotches paling to peach; the clerk in the liquor store again had teeth like paperwhites, the testicles cleaved to the penis, shoulders squared, and a pudding of baby fat spilled over checkered shorts.

But Lastivka he'd known as a girl.

Scared her even then. Her father's difficult brother, in town briefly on some mission (meeting with Trotsky? Lenin?). She stood in the door between hall and living room, clutching a stuffed butterfly, a six-year-old with tight blonde curls glinting in the gas light, lower lip quivering, scared to approach until he dropped to his knees and meowed meekly. "Would you like a cream puff?"

Food was opium, penicillin, ambrosia. She took after her mother. He composed himself. How many years did one get to practice being human before the part felt natural?

"A *matzoh* would be ample."

She brought an apple.

His family's behavior bothered him. They assured him he was a superb specimen, destined or doomed to another decade at least. But he knew better from their faces. They gawked as though he were already drained, embalmed, rouged. They couldn't help being curious: so this was what it looked like. The corpses they'd seen in the war had faded. Their faces revealed an eagerness.

Why didn't they ask him questions?

Mine is not a normal nature, Stefan thought.

To his family he was an aged diplomat, *un homme du monde,* former resident of the City of Light, maybe a traitor.

He wanted to explain what happened to a man, things he'd told no one. How strange it was to live in a world where no one knew or cared about Katherine Schratt or mourned the suicides of Crown Prince Rudolf and Princess Stephanie (on account of that Baroness Vetsera bitch) or recollected the stories about Princess Pauline Metternich's parties, the groping and sighs in the coat rooms during the charity balls, the Linzertorte at the Imperial Hotel. Once archdukes cruised the streets in crystal caleches. The emperor rode through the Prater in a carriage of gold and glass, drawn by eight grays, surrounded by soldiers and gendarmes with ivy sprigs in their helmets.

Years of regimen and luxurious form.

He turned twenty-one in 1916, the year the zeppelins attacked Paris. Year of the Battle of Verdun, the Easter Rebellion, the first tank. The year Emperor Franz Joseph finally cashed it in, three decades too late, people said. Rasputin was murdered that year. Max Planck took the Nobel for giving the world the quantum theory, which, more than half a century later, Stefan still did not understand. What had any of this to do with him? That was the decade he was not sober for one single day.

Later he worked at the house in Marseille. The girls would gladly have arranged a party for his fortieth but, under the circumstances, it seemed silly.

In 1946 he celebrated his birthday in a displaced persons camp in Germany.

His seventy-fifth occurred around the time he was finishing out his tenure as a sales clerk at Woolworth's. He had a party, but his heart wasn't in it.

Smile, he said to himself. If nothing else, we'll out-smile these Americans. Goodwill. Goodwill will get us through.

Bo bounded up the stairs. Sometimes Stefan helped him with his history; other times the boy sat on the bed while they leafed through stamp albums.

"*Abu Dhabi,*" Stefan said, "like the opening of an Arabian charm."

They played the Abu Dhabi game.

"You understand, I am doing this because my heart is heavy with boredom."

Bo bowed his head, humming.

"Hobbies are for the defeated," he said to the boy.

"Once I believed I'd love old age, free of what Aeschylus called the madness of sex. Misplaced idealism on my part. I'd much rather be riding a horse through a dark forest, having randy thoughts, or rolling in the grass with a village girl. Village girls are the best."

"Don't tease!"

He crumpled. A man who'd wasted his life. Suddenly serious, he said, "Claim your place, son, claim your place. Don't be shy. The world is not that fragile. It's waiting for you to make your mark. Claim your place. The world is waiting. Claim it.

"Remember that you're here because your parents stood up to the people the Americans were opposing. Remember that. Someone took an interest in your parents' case, not because of who they were, but because of the side they were on. They were on the right side. Son, that side stood for property, individual responsibility. You've got to chose what you believe in. It decides everything else. Remember why you're here in the first place."

Then they played their stamp game. Each made up a country for which he designed a stamp. Bo's place had long nights for dreams, sunny days lasting decades for playing near the river, warm snow so you could sled in your bathing suit, and no school. Stefan wanted women with perfumed hair and low voices. "You can't draw low voices," Bo pointed out.

"Or warm snow," Stephan countered.

"Come down here and help me," Lastivka called. The boy obeyed his mother.

If you are careless enough to lose a country and a continent, you deserve what you get.

The afternoon light, sifted by the pines, crept along the floor. The leaves of the maranta again rose while he wasn't looking.

Good-bye, sun.

Other visitors included Claudia, with whom he'd worked at Woolworth's.

Her dark skin reminded him of Mrs. Glick. Wet eyes he swam in.

"How's married life?"

"Another stage."

"You make it sound like one of the stations of the cross."

"Don't laugh, Mr. Z."

"No, no. Only you know you should have married me." He wanted to pinch her. "I'm dying, sweetheart."

She turned serious, and he regretted having spoken.

"It's no big deal. It couldn't happen at a better time. Look, you know the story about Buddha and the mustard seed?" He pinched her cheek. "A woman who lost her child begged the Buddha to bring the girl back. He told her if she could bring him a mustard seed from just one house where nobody had ever died, he'd do it."

John Blacklips, the mailman, stopped over a few times. He was a Penobscot Indian, from Maine. After his wife drowned while canoeing in the Orono River, he'd left the reservation. For some reason he called Stefan "professor." Lately, he'd been missing "his people."

"Look at me," Stefan told him, "I'm stuck with these Ukes day and night. Suffocating. At least at Woolworth's there was air. Here it's the same. Listen, they can't wait for me to die."

John nodded. "I understand, professor. But the light, and the voices. They just aren't the same. It's Maine I miss as much as anything. I tell myself that people are people everywhere. But my heart says not all people are your people."

"I know," he said, staring at the *Odalisque*.

The variety.

"What did you do in the war?"

"I was in a camp."

"During World War I?"

"I was seven, fighting with my brother."

"I left my people long ago. I couldn't leave fast enough. I hated them, hated their smell, their habits, their stupidity. All of it poison."

Downstairs they argued.

"I won't let you."

"Who do you think you are to say such things?"

"It's my money."

"*You* clean! *You* scrub Stefan, the dog. King of what? No place at all."

Stefan's dentures ground against each other. What good had he done anyone? Even with Bo. He told himself he was helping by giving the boy geography lessons, but really it was Bo who entertained him. He'd promised his brother he'd care for them, and he'd tried. But mostly things happened the other way.

He put down his tea, rubbed the spider bite on his wrist. He'd wasted a century. Not likely he'd have another. But the insurance policy. Small, nearly nothing, but it would buy Bo some years of college.

He dabbed his left eye with a monogramed hankie.

Orange syrup on the stove.

In December Lastivka cooked. For three weeks the house smelled of fried onions, boiled cabbage, and gingerbread. Tin upon tin of cookies piled up on the dining room table. The floor in the kitchen was dusted with flour. She worked as though the newly discovered eleventh commandment declared: *Thou shalt cook.*

He looked at the plants, the jade, the kalanchoe, the ficus lyrata. Had there been a greenhouse in Paris, and his hands on Lida's breasts, the smell of her hair, and the cymbidiums?

In his day he'd plied himself with pleasures, soaked in the world like a plant. From the first suck on his mother's nipple to his stalking Mrs. Glick to Mathilda and Lida, his only interest in life had been his own pleasure.

Egoist. Delusional. Like his father, the priest.

He would redeem himself. Not himself alone. His whole intolerable race! Tomorrow, in one radiant gesture, he would reclaim all, his past, the history of his people!

He lay on top of the blankets while rain collected in rivulets on the roof.

He was naked, crawling through space beneath a lattice of stars when a woman's voice whispered his name. He looked over his shoulder. Then he began falling. He dropped a long time before finally landing in his old bed in Rozdorizha while outside snow swirled like shredded stars. He heard the church bell ring even though he was dead.

He blinked at the Christmas lights framing a house across the street. He rose, slipped on his blue woolen robe, and limped to the bathroom.

A horse flew over the garage. Strafed by rain, mane raging, the weathervane raced north-northeast through the night.

He thought of his uncle arriving on horseback one Christmas and his mother calling in her sons—Ihor, Zenon, and himself—and announcing that their father was dead. On Christmas Eve her gift to them: nothing less than the truth. Ihor, of course, didn't understand.

And it was years before Stefan found out how his old man died. By then the story seemed comic.

And there was a horse in the field the day he and Orko went to see Mrs. Glick. Mrs. Glick, who pierced the Zabobon cloth like a needle.

———————

That summer the locusts got sick. They died suddenly, in air, by the tens of thousands. Their brittle bodies crackled underfoot and clogged the sewers like leaves. Old Ivan gathered up sackfuls, enameled them, and later sold them as Christmas ornaments.

"You know who Christopher Columbus is?" Orko asked Stefan.

They had just learned that, according to the Bible, in 1492 the world was supposed to end.

They were sitting under a willow outside the schoolhouse. Recess lasted as long as it took for Mr. Krawchuk to go to the tavern and back.

"Of course."

"Then follow me."

Orko led him down streets bordered with poplars, past the sagging bridge, near the place where old man Voroch, who claimed he'd seen devils dancing the *hopak* outside the church, had been roasted by lightning.

"Where are we going?" Stefan asked.

"To see another continent. Another world."

They arrived at a house surrounded by a white picket fence, above which peered the black faces of sunflowers.

The air swarmed with bees, meadowlarks, cabbage moths. No locusts.

Across from the house stretched a field splattered with poppies. A lone black mare munched the grass.

"Are we going to steal the horse?"

Quiet, Orko signaled, and crept through the meadow to an agitated apple tree, which he climbed nimbly, and Stefan followed, settling on a branch near the top. First he saw only grass and a willow. Then his heart turned and he broke into a sweat. He clutched the branch tighter.

Beyond the willow, full in the sun, framed by a brown blanket and burnt grass, lay a naked woman.

"Who is she?"

"Mrs. Glick."

She lay on her back, legs splayed toward the boys so they could see the wild moss covering the fork, breasts capped with brown poppies, skin gleaming like moistened mahogany burnished with sunlight. Her face was hidden under a straw bonnet until she sat up.

It was the most beautiful face he'd ever seen. She blinked into the fence, feeling their eyes. Instead of covering herself, she opened her legs wider and swiped the sweat from her cheeks and dropped her hands between her thighs where something—a blade of grass, a dead bee—had lodged.

Black flies feasted on the boys' scabbed legs. Their shadows on the dirt road blurred and twined with the branches. They stayed until Orko noticed a wagon hobbling along, and then they raced across the meadow, grass blackening, the few remaining locusts meditating on their sins as the sun set.

He returned to the lookout often. Twice he contrived visits to the furniture store, hoping to see Mrs. Glick clothed. Passing the varnished cabinets and chairs, he sweated, scanning the store nervously. He found only fat Mr. Glick, who wore a diamond ring on each finger of both hands. He kept returning to the field long after the days had shortened, and the only naked things outside were the trees. He left Mrs. Glick out of Saturday's confessions. He felt guilty. But whom could he tell? Orko? The damned cannot absolve the damned.

Years later he learned his mother had left his father because of her. And that his father, a priest, had died of syphilis.

———

Snow and insomnia slowly erased the boundaries between worlds.

Early that morning Stefan gets up and puts on a shirt that gleams like cream in the lamplight. His bow tie. His double-breasted gray suit. The gray wool overcoat with most of the buttons missing. Buries a pipe and Sobrani in his pocket, grabs the dolphin-handled cane, his neatly creased fedora, and descends.

Downstairs, people everywhere. Nephews, grandnieces, ancient discolored cousins clinging lichenlike to couches. The old man moves slowly yet efficiently through the chaos. He is already something of a ghost. Yuri curls at the foot of the Christmas tree. Stefan picks up the phone.

"What are you doing, Uncle?" Lastivka asks, sealing a bowl of *kutia* under plastic wrap.

"Going to Red Brook," he replies.

"Don't you want to go with Eddie and the kids to the

mall?" She looks puzzled. Red Brook is the Ukrainian cemetery where the entire family has its considerable plot, bought and paid for.

"No, I don't think so," he smiles, heading for the door.

A child screams. Lastivka calls out, "Darka!"

On the couch the twins argue, "After all, it's a German holiday, this Christmas, with presents . . . "

He will never have to listen to their nonsense again.

He shakes his head as though emptying his ear of water, pouring out the family he's waded through. A sad lot, anywhere you look. He wishes he could say something to them—Pavlo, Orest, and Ihor, Anton, Olga, Yarka, and Arkady and Lastivka—something, a scrap of wisdom to heal them. But he remembers his mission. He nods, mumbling to himself, and walks on.

Waiting in the cold for the cab, he looks at the pine towering above the house. It was a sapling when they moved here a decade ago.

They fixed up the garage, tamed the garden, painted the house, installed a new boiler, planted a cherry orchard on the east side.

Today the yard and the house look as derelict as they did when the family arrived.

He takes a shovel from the garage. In one hand, his cane; in the other, the shovel.

Inside the cab, he pulls out his pipe but doesn't fill it. Enough just to hold it. Soon the taxi's driving west on

Route 22. And Stefan does not object. He doesn't object to anything.

Route 22, with its thousands of neon-lit stores, shoe emporiums alongside lumberyards and amusement parks.

His mission focuses him. He turns from the window and draws a letter from his pocket. It's dated from three years ago and begins *Dear Father*.

The salutation startles him now as much as then. He never married. The boy — but the letter was from an old man near seventy — was Lida's. Lida, whom he loved in Paris between wars.

And all that work gone into his metaphysics of marriage. He will be better off underground.

The driver says he hasn't seen a storm like this since the blizzard of '48. Stefan hardly hears him. He's already deep in the other world. When the car stops, he looks puzzled. A flat tire. Ah. He will get out.

He lives among strangers. He wishes there were at least one person, a wife, even a priest, who really knew him. He smiles, shakes the snow off his hat, and now there's wind, so he reties the scarf, which he stuffed into his pocket at the last minute.

"These bolts are glued . . . "

The man speaks so confidently about the material world. He's an American, carrying none of the burden of the past. His hates and loves are instinctual. He may be bald and thin, but his spirit is large. Why, Americans even embrace Russians. What do they care about what the poet Deke calls the tribal wars of Europe?

He'll miss Claudia, from Woolworth's. John Black-lips, the mailman.

The tire slips from the cabbie's hands. Snow erases everything. May as well be on a lake in Siberia as on a small highway off Route 22 in northern New Jersey on Christmas Eve in the middle of a blizzard.

Das ist ein Schwindel—as Lenin said when he understood the way the working classes were cheated. Everyone bilked them: the aristocrats, the merchants, their own children. Workers sweated their souls away in hopes of gaining heaven while the rest of the world ate the fruits of their labors. But to Stefan the phrase meant even more. It is a swindle. It: what? Life. The world. All of it. A swindle? It is a cosmic hallucination. The only reason for playing by the rules is to gain a better understanding of the rules. But there's no understanding the game itself. Identity is a lie. History is a lie. Psychology the history of lies. And so on. Up and down do not exist. They are categories created by "up" to keep "down" down. Einstein, speaking in the language of physics, said the same thing. It burst open a door. We are freer than we know or want to know. We create ourselves. But there are so few guidelines. We're barely capable of making a good bouillabaisse. We shouldn't hope for too much in the way of humans.

He remembers in detail the last time he and Lida made love, but he doesn't remember the greenhouse. He remembers her breasts above the tight blue gown and her tongue on his cheek . . .

How ashamed I am of my life. I won't embarrass you with my confession. My sins would take too long. But I can't sleep and

I can hardly speak because I am so full of shame for the way I lived . . . and now there's nothing I can do.

"Sorry, pal, we're not going anywhere today . . . "

———

Somberly, as though the night were a saturnalia of sadness, they filtered in to the Vorogs' dining room for the Christmas Eve dinner. First came Blind Peter and Teta Vera, followed by Edward and Lilka Zaremba, and the twins ("It's a German habit, this exchanging of gifts . . . ," George whined to Pavlo), then Valentyn, Darka, other children, and a half-dozen adults related to the Vorogs by blood or need.

Lastivka raced between the dining room and the kitchen until Lilka said, "Oh sit, everything's perfect."

"What did the moon say about my presents, Teta Lilka?"

"Wonderful things."

"Like what?"

They heard Stefan. Back late from his aborted mission, he'd put on his gray suit, a clean starched shirt, and a bow tie resembling a second moustache. His sparse hair curled on his shoulders, and he leaned heavily on the dolphin-handled cane. His only souvenir was his red nose. He sneezed worse than ever.

Bo felt the room grow crowded.

Everyone sank into a trance. On the white tablecloth, next to the candelabrum, sat a tureen brimming with borscht dappled with haloes of oil. The gold rings reminded him of the eyes of the carp Lastivka scaled earlier. Death owned the first part of the night.

In a voice sepulchral as Deacon Procak's intoning the Acts of the Apostles, Stefan spoke, "Let us remember those no longer with us . . . "

Bo saw snow-covered mountains swell up around the room. Wind shivered the candles.

Each name conjured a face. He watched Jadviga the cook chase a goose around her great-grandfather's courtyard, catch it, snap its neck; Jews, among them the legendary Mrs. Glick, herded into the square by the Nazis; Madame Poprovska riding a white horse through a park in Paris; Ihor taken by the police; Zenon shot by the Germans.

Tonight the old man had stories he needed to tell. For once, he didn't hold back.

He talked about Fedor, who stumbled home late one Christmas night, for which his wife rewarded him by sticking a knife through his neck. Then the bombing of Lviv. And Vienna. Somewhere Stefan refused to go to the shelter when the siren sounded. He lay in a tub reading when the bomb broke the wall, shooting an arrow into his side. At the piano sat greasy Meister Rakovsky, said to have betrayed his country twice, first to the Germans, then to the Russians, but who emigrated anyway, Lord knew why. He'd been Lastivka's piano teacher at the DP camp. He could improvise for hours until it seemed the spirit of Liszt commanded his body. And it was this gift, Stefan pointed out, of a mind able to resolve the incongruities of experience into harmony, that betrayed him.

The moral, he added—gazing toward Bo, who seemed the only one listening—being that no one gift alone, no matter how prodigious, makes a man good.

The longer he spoke, the livelier he became. His memory played a crude fugue. No one could follow it. The others had long ago dried their tears, beat back their black thoughts. They were ready to breathe in the present. Arkady yawned, and Lilka picked up a spoon and tapped tepidly on her soup bowl. But the old man brimmed with ghosts. They swelled inside him like sails luffing the wind. He laughed, pinched the speartips of his moustache, and told everyone how his brother Zenon set out one morning to find the easel on which the sky rested. Bo saw a frame harboring snatches of sky above the table. Stefan's voice raced on the way music must have poured from Meister Rakovsky's fingers. Lviv, Peremyshl, Berchtesgaden: names and people, once divided by decades and miles, suddenly chafing like clothes in the closet. Stefan had worn, and worn out, them all.

Then Lastivka placed a hand on her uncle's shoulder and he woke up. He blinked, traced his tongue over his lips, recited the Hail Mary and Our Father, said the benediction, and passed around the plate of honeyed holy bread.

The meal began.

He awoke to a new noise: plop, plop. A leak in the roof, water collecting in a depression in the floor at the foot of his bed. He looked at the *Odalisque* lounging in oriental splendor on his wall. Lida's cheeks. He pulled the blue sheet up to his neck. Crisp, newly washed. He thought of the *bandurists* at Lastivka's wedding, of the hot dogs eaten outside Ellis Island, the coffee-colored water slapping the boats in the harbor; Martine's soft breasts in the cool September breeze; of his father, whose funeral he'd missed, walking near the Simplon Pass in Switzerland; at the Italian border, cowbells clanging behind him, then coffee in the restaurant in Brigg and the waitress with her frank smile and large hips. And in the deepening silence, after decades surrounded by the noises of others, of cities, of wars, he began to hear another voice. At first it was very soft and blurred. Then it grew clearer. It was the voice of another self. Life played to an audience of one. Should he put in his dentures? Idiot Ihor arrested and had disappeared—according to Zenon, untraceable. Nothing dies and parts of me will also live. Parts of me. Wasted life. Addict, sensualist, pawn of earthly powers. If Eros couldn't save them, then what? Yet. Even in dying a sweetness. He regretted only moments of anger, of cruelty. Let each enter calmly the kingdom of dust.

————

His mother moves in soft white light but he can't fix her. Everything dances. The yellow hutch blurs into the blue wall. The photo of God bleeds from the frame. The fever freaks his brain with colors and sharp thoughts that melt. He feels this way at school sometimes when he looks at words, and they are hard and bulge like mountains, and he forgets what they mean: then he merely adores their shape. Other times the words are clear as brook water and he sees through them to the humped toad and the orange fish, and the water tumbles him forward. *Why?* There seems no reason. Now his soldiers scream at him. They sit in their camp on the floor. They bleed; they sigh. His mother will help the broken one find his arm. Brain of limestone, pond muck, heron, copperhead. Brain of summer. Summer brain. He never wants to go to school again. Billy Weir is a bastard. He isn't sure what the word means; he's just guessing on the wet blue sheet; damp with fever and sweat and his nose alerted to rubbing alcohol. Isopropyl! Once he and Rick talked about girls and he told him about wrestling with Darka. He heard someone laughing outside the window by the mulberry. His mother sits on the edge of the bed holding a cup of tea laced with lemon and honey. She smells like sheets doused in mulberry water. She runs her fingers through his hair. His soul begins to dissolve, his face is not his, he's left his body and hangs in the air near the cloudy lamp fixture, a moth beating above his mother bending over him. In the background his father's voice breaks in. He's near, winking. Bo loves him even though he yells. He's brought the saucer-shaped paperweight. Uncle Stefan is dead. He stands the thing on its inch-thick edge and twirls it. It gyroscopes — a ballerina or iron marble rounding the rim of a pan. Slowly it whirls lower, the sound of its falling slowing until it is a heavy noise. His brain is pierced with white-hot needles. Once his mother said if he spoke English, she'd prick his tongue with a needle. But he loves English because the new words have a taste, and the old ones don't. They make the house better. A chair has a cushion but *krislo* is a hard wood. His mother asks if he wants a story, and he does, but his eyes are heavy and his head aches from counting all the soldiers. His mother sings and he closes his eyes and sleeps.

———————

Bo walks to the bed where the body lies tucked to the neck in a Greek blue sheet, his long head framed by a blue pillow case. He looks like a shell on the ocean floor. Bo thinks of walking with him on the beach in Wildwood and in the woods in the Carpathians. He still has a fever. He senses the other presences, vaguely hears his mother whispering to Teta Vera who goes out and comes back. He gets closer, smells the sourness, like moldy bread. He wants to put a hand on his forehead, to touch death. He doesn't dare. He feels he's been in the sun a long time. He's transparent. It's as though he himself had died. Maybe the old man has some last thing to tell him and has spirited him away from the others. Stefan no longer speaks in the old way. He can't explain, in his deep and precise voice, about the coal and naphtha regions south of Lviv, or joke about a mysterious past, or place that long-fingered hand on Bo's shoulder and squeeze, or talk through pipe smoke about Paris and some girl.

Lace curtains puff and fall like lungs. The house breathes, and the priest crowds in, crowding him out.

———————

He is buried at Red Brook. The funeral doesn't go as planned. The grave digger falls asleep so when they get there they have to wait for him.

Father Brodin swings his censer. The mourners, John Blacklips and Claudia among them, breathe in the incense.

A month passes before Lastivka realizes he's gone.

It's as though his death took place outside her field of vision. She wept of course as the coffin was lowered and the mourners sang *Vichnaya Pamyat*. But who really thinks he'll be remembered forever? All dissolve in a solution of dust and rose petals and rain. At the reception she gazed at the guests, friends from the old country. But all afternoon it was as though she'd been somewhere else. One night, after making love for the first time in months, Arkady asked her what she was thinking. "I'm always partly somewhere else," she'd confided.

She realized it while polishing the dining room table. An almond torte was browning in the oven. Grief. Sudden. Determined. Her heart seemed to squeeze out her lungs: she couldn't breathe. She hurried downstairs to talk to Lilka. But Lilka had already left for the hospital. She tried phoning a friend from the church sodality. No answer. She paced through the house picking up chairs, putting them down, twisting the curtain, unfurling.

Bo watched. When he asked what was wrong, Lastivka answered, "Call a cab."

"Where are we going?"

"Red Brook," she told the driver.

Decades ago she spent hundreds of hours in cemeteries reading Steinbeck and Lägerloff and others.

She missed her ghosts.

On the headstone a Byzantine cross rose between the two significant dates. Beside it stretched the plots reserved for Arkady and herself.

It was bird hour when she pulled the trowel from her pocket and began digging.

She knew nothing about Stefan's last scheme.

The winter sun lay stranded somewhere behind a slate sky. A choir of starlings, settled in the oak, chirped loudly. The earth, after a dry month, was hard and hungry stone. She jabbed and jabbed. Why had she prayed, why had she bothered? Nothing helped. She thought of her father, Zenon. What a strange man he'd been; how she loved his ghostly visits. In life his touch had been gentle as a cat's. She remembered one morning when Natalka was sick and Jadviga out, and she needed to get ready for school, which meant braiding her sandy blonde hair. At his daughter's request, Zenon took up the brush. His fingers fell through her hair like rain through reeds. They were standing before a mirror. She saw him so clearly. She looked at his eyes, which behind the thick bifocals were as distant as when he sat in his study smoking his pipe and reading a book. His hands moved gracefully. What was the last thing he'd said to her? That he'd see her in a week? Another man who lied.

Stefan became her father. He was unreachable at the end. Something had been bothering him since Christmas. One afternoon she brought him his soup and found him shredding papers and dropping them into a bag which he asked her to burn.

Then she recalled the old woman on the boat who said they would suffer horribly because they'd forgotten to bring their ghosts. But they had not forgotten them. She'd done all she could to make friends with them.

She stared around, wild, blind to the squirrel watching her from under the naked forsythia.

Bo wandered among the gravestones awhile.

Finally he went to the public phone at the entrance and called Arkady at work.

By the time he arrived, Lastivka had gouged a hole a foot wide and two deep, the moon was up, and she was ready to leave.

At home she shook off her shoes and sank onto the couch. She hugged her coat around her.

The next morning, on his way to the bathroom, the boy found his mother and father, fully dressed, locked together, curled on the floor.

Wind sweeps the branches. Far away, a child cries.

Toor Zabobon opens his eyes. They are moons. They light the ground several feet in front of him. He yawns. Bats fly out of his mouth. He scratches his black hairy face, and his tongue, long as a snake, leaps out and traces his mustache, stiff as a juniper. He licks the fringe of his beard, which falls below his knees and tangles with the grass.

He is hungry. That's the first thing. His one arm feels among the top branches of the tree for the bird's nest he's sniffed out. His fingers close over the robin, which wakes only after it is deep down his throat.

Sated, Toor stands. His eyes drill into the second-story window, level with his chin.

And who is this?

He bends nearer, breath rattling the panes. Two

shapes cling to each other on the floor. He doesn't recognize either.

He straightens up and looks around. What small houses these people live in. Weird branches growing from their roof tops. And so many windows. What do they do when it snows? He breathes deeply and tries to think, but thinking doesn't come easily to him.

His tongue plays over a bone lodged between his teeth. His body itches. Has he always been this hairy? Or did the brush take root while he slept?

Something is not right. He peers into the window again, studies the faces. Crude, but good-hearted, he thinks, looking at the snoring Arkady. And Lastivka's face is familiar. A good woman. Bless them both. And to think they're relations — but where did that idea come from? Sometimes words rush into his head straight from the air itself.

And where is Olha, his wife? He remembers the Tartars. He feels around his neck for the skull cups but they're gone. He sniffs the air, his nose crinkling like a monstrous caterpillar. Poisons, he thinks. The air is filled with them as though nearby some enemy burned evil herbs.

He glimpses a squirrel. His hand shoots out like a hawk.

Yes. Hunger. And then what?

The place is familiar. He's seen it before. This isn't Rozdorizha, but he's been here.

He looks down the corridor of centuries behind him, and he looks ahead. He sees the faces of the children that were born to his children; and he remembers his mother, smiles; sees the gaunt face of his grandmother, frowns, and he claws backwards through the brush, pushing past pines, the needles poking his scaly skin, and he looks at the ground. His toes are growing into roots.

He peers into the other window. A boy, who should be getting ready for school, tosses in a dream.

He leans forward. What is the child dreaming?

Toor snorts. A shape hardly human moves in the garden. A being, all force and appetite and love, gazes into the window of the house in Free Fall, New Jersey. His feet sink deep into the earth. He scratches his chin and looks to the sky as though he expects to see through the clouds and the darkness beyond. Bark slowly covers his skin. He throws back his head and laughs.

Acknowledgments

This novel, and certainly this novelist, owe at the very least their lives to a few friends: Alex, Peter and Lynn, Sharon and John, Tom, Bill and Beverly, Stuart and Karen, Jeffrey, and Tom (in no particular order). My thanks, too, to the places that helped the writing get done: Cranford, Peterborough, Provincetown, Cambridge, Leverett, Ryegate, and Bedford. Finally, my abiding gratitude to my editor, Fiona McCrae.

Parts of this book appeared in earlier versions in *Mss, The Gettysburg Review,* and *The Denver Quarterly.*